At seventeen, Lucy Tan was offered the lead in the school musical *Queen of the May*. She turned it down in favour of working on set design with her beloved teacher, August Herron. Later, she wishes she hadn't. As she grows older, Lucy realises her life calls for a lot of compromises. She works at her dream job, but since that means being off the grid and unavailable for half of every year, sustaining a romance is difficult. *Catch and release* is her solution, but that's a compromise, too. What she needs is a man she can put in cold storage . . . or maybe one with an off switch.

She doesn't find one like that, but she does find Paris, who is sexy, gorgeous and devoted to her pleasure. She can't exactly take him home to meet her parents, though. For one thing, he lives in fairyland, where he spends most of his time attending to the needs of lonely women. For another, he has a weird aversion to wearing clothes.

But Lucy is determined. This is her life, and this time, she's going to play the leading role.

Queen of the May
Copyright © 2020 Lark Westerly
ISBN: 978-1-4874-2860-0
Cover art by Martine Jardin

Published by eXtasy Books Inc or
Devine Destinies, an imprint of eXtasy Books Inc

Look for us online at:
www.eXtasybooks.com or www.devinedestinies.com

Queen of the May
A Fairy in the Bed

By

Lark Westerly

Author's Note:

Ever since completing *The Pear Tree,* the love story of Nelis Winter and Xavier Partridge, I've wondered what became of Nelis's sensible friend, Lucy Tan. I knew she was still working at the Ferris Island camp, but what else was going on in her life? Then there was Paris, whose mother was a water maid and whose father was human. He was devoted to his best friend, London, but now London was a family man . . . on the face of it, Lucy and Paris are an unlikely match, but as I wrote their story, I realised they were also a *perfect* match.

The *Fairy in the Bed* series features a sprawling cast of characters who wander in and out of one another's stories.

Queen of the May stands alone, but you may recognise some of the characters and settings.

Lucy Tan, our heroine, appeared as the sensible friend of Nelis Winter in *The Pear Tree.* August Herron, Xavier "Bird Boy" Partridge, Otto Fairling, Diversity High, Ferris Island and the Pear Tree pub all appear in that book, too.

Paris appears in a small part in *Love Began at Christmas,* and also, along with his friend London, in the *Counterpoint* books. His mother, Fee, appears in *Calico Calypso,* as well as in other stories, and the falls is a regular setting.

Mama Tam and her family appear in *Pisky Business,* and in other stories.

Asha is from *Honey and the Harvest Hob.*

Lore Mor Arlodh and Xanthe are from *Xanthe and the Seaman.*

Finally, Yvanne Skipton Peckerdale, and her husband, Quinn, who cameo right at the end of the story, featured in *Love Began at Christmas.*

PART ONE: DIVERSITY HIGH SCHOOL
2011-12

CHAPTER ONE: LUCY'S CHOICE

Lucy Tan, 2011, Diversity High

When she was sixteen, Lucy Tan tumbled into love with August Herron.

In the classroom, she spent long dreamy periods learning every line of his face, watching his deft movements, and bathing in his air of sparkling enthusiasm.

She learned to split her attention, so half of her was intelligent, studious Lucy, applying herself to projects and assignments, answering questions and volunteering well-formed opinions. The other half spent those same classes inventing scenarios where she helped him with something important, and he kissed her and then they —

And then he'd be mortified because teachers aren't allowed to kiss students.

Okay, so she helped him, and he gave her a special smile.

Class was ending. She was vaguely aware of Nelis Winter packing away her notes across the aisle.

Someone rustled busily away behind her. She smelled a waft of marmalade.

One of the fay . . . and probably a full blood.

Special smile . . .

God, Lucy, what are you? Nine? Special smile indeed.

A long, slow meeting of eyes?

God, Lucy, you're so —

She couldn't think what she was.

Desperate.

"Lucy?"

Oh God!

He'd spoken to her, and she hadn't heard. She cast her mind back, hoping some residual echo might tell her what he'd said.

"Lucy?" August Herron gave her a quizzical smile. Her name sounded lovely in his soft voice, with the little upwards tilt.

"I'm sorry, Mister Herron. I was thinking about something else."

I should say, Master Herron. *That way you'd know I know what you are.*

Lu-cy, don't be an idiot. He doesn't care what you know. He barely even bothers to glamour his ears. A quarter of this class has at least one fairy in the family pot . . .

Mercifully, he just smiled and repeated the question, coming down from his desk On High to stand beside her as the classroom emptied around them.

Ohhhh, you smell so good! Broad bean flowers . . .

"Are you up for the lead in *Queen of the May?*"

She got up in an undignified scramble, feeling sweat forming between her shoulders.

Don't smile too broadly. It makes your eyes disappear.

He wasn't a tall man, but even standing, the top of her head was about level with his chin.

"Why?" She knew she sounded wary, but she had to get this right. He didn't teach drama, so what reason could he have for wanting to know?

"If you are, then the best of luck. I think you'd nail it."

She blinked.

"But if you're not, or if you're going for a smaller part, I'd like you to help me with set design."

"I'd love to."

"Great. Let me know as soon as you decide."

Lucy had already auditioned. She'd been singing and

dancing since she was four, and she knew she was good. The musical was the story of a modern girl who found herself in Merrie England, where, over her protestations of sexism and exploitation, she was crowned Queen of the May and used her influence to improve the lot of the village maidens. It was fluffy and dated, but it had lots of parts, and Bess, the heroine, had some amusing solos. The finale, called *Beat of My Own Drum*, would really weed out the competition. Bess had to carry a strong melody line above a chorus of thirty singing a different tune.

Despite her powerful singing voice, Lucy knew she had little hope of playing Bess, who spent one whole soliloquy pointing out that she *stood taller than all the guys*.

She had run through the scene at the auditions to predictable jeers from boys, who said *yes, if they were on their knees* . . .

It hurt. She wanted to be Bess.

Grow up, Lucy. No matter how hard you work, you won't grow a head taller and be big, blonde and beautiful. *You'll be cast as a village urchin . . . or maybe the comedy pedlar girl. Being passed over because you're not a good-enough singer or actor is one thing, but being passed over because of your genes is worse. You can improve your skills, but if you're short and mostly Chinese, you're short . . . and mostly Chinese.*

Now, of course, she was glad she wouldn't get the part. Helping Master August Herron with set design? *Yes, please.* She was dancing on air, and she wondered why she hadn't said *yes* right away.

Drama was the last class of the day. After the siren wailed, Jenny Shackleton said, "Lucy, a word."

"Yes, Ms Shackleton." She stayed behind as Miffy and Melanie Smith, the ill-assorted cousins, clumped noisily past her.

"You're in for it now, Tan," Melanie muttered, more in hope than from conviction.

Lucy frowned. The teachers of Diversity High seldom told

one off in public. They were much more likely to ask for help with a trifling task . . . and then unleash on the luckless student.

But I can't be in trouble. I haven't done anything. Or am I in trouble for fibbing about the audition? I didn't tell Mister Herron I hadn't auditioned. I said . . .

Her thoughts tangled.

Ms Shackleton shooed out the cousins, who showed signs of hopeful lingering, and closed the door firmly behind them.

"Am I in trouble, Ms Shackleton?"

Jenny Shackleton smiled. "Not at all. I just wanted to give you the heads up before I finalise the cast list . . . I'd like you to play Bess."

For a moment, the words made no sense, and then Lucy felt a surge of astonished delight. Then she remembered lovely Mister Herron and the sets.

She couldn't do both. All sections of work on the Year Eleven musical occupied the same time-blocks.

She gave herself a few seconds to envisage each scenario and came to the only decision she could countenance.

"No, thanks, Ms Shackleton."

Jenny Shackleton's face, which had been benevolent and smiling, blanked in amazement.

A penny dropped with a small, almost audible, *chink.*

Offering the part to me is some kind of policy statement.

"I'm nothing like the way Bess describes herself in the songs."

Ms Shackleton relaxed. "Oh, I think we can get around that. Maybe we can put you up on a table when you sing *stand taller,* or you might sing *smaller* rather than *taller?* And *intelligent and dutiful* instead of *big, blonde and beautiful.* Yes, why not? We don't want to emphasise the popular concept of physical beauty."

No, we don't, do we. Even though the script clearly does it in an ironic way.

You don't truly believe I'm best for the part. You're just making a point by casting a small, dark girl of Asian appearance as a Queen of the May and maybe sticking up two fingers at those idiotic boys with their down on their knees *comments.*

Well, I'm no one's point and no one's poster person.

She said, stiffly, "I don't think so, thank you. There's still the *England's Rose* song, and I don't think someone who looks the way I do would have been crowned as May Queen in Merrie England, do you? This reeks of *positive discrimination* to me."

Ms Shackleton flushed a deep, plum red and said, "That's a very cynical view, Lucy. Here at Diversity, we believe in absolute equality."

"But we're not equal, Ms Shackleton. Some of us are better than others."

She meant to expand on her theory about the need for the quintet of talent, dedication, genetic disposition, environment and desire, but Ms Shackleton was going all tight-jawed.

"If that's your attitude, I'll withdraw the offer."

"I could fit in one of the smaller parts," Lucy ventured.

"They're already cast."

"But you'll have to upgrade someone . . . or . . ."

"Thank you, Lucy. I don't need any more of your condescension."

Lucy hurried out, cheeks stinging, pretending not to see Melanie and Miffy still lingering.

The sting faded as she strode around the visual arts classroom.

August Herron wasn't there.

Of course. He has appointments from three-thirty every day.

As well as teaching visual arts and PD, Mister Herron was the school counsellor. It was only a few minutes after three, and the screen was still open in the little privacy alcove, so she went to tap on his office door.

"Come in."

She opened the door.

"You're a bit early, but I'll be with you in a minute. Help yourself to coffee—" He looked up with a professional smile from the papers he was sorting. "Oh, Lucy. I thought you were my three-thirty." His smile turned genuine. "What can I do for you?"

She glanced behind him at the wall full of cups and mugs. Flowers and cartoons, birds, slogans, dogs... she was tempted to take him up on the offer of coffee, but she didn't want to get mixed up with his three-thirty.

"I came to tell you I've decided. I'm not in the musical... well, not in a role."

I won't even make the chorus, if Ms Shackleton can help it.

"I hope you're not too disappointed."

"Oh, no! I'd much rather help you." She sought for something more grown-up. "I mean... realistically, I'm never going to make a career out of acting, but a set design project is good experience for a lot of jobs."

"You see yourself in this area of work, then?"

She hadn't, but now she did. Again, she sought for the best spin.

"I haven't decided yet, but I'd like broad experience in creation and innovation... maybe even teaching or organising projects."

He nodded. "That's how I came to be in my position. My *two* positions. I'd love to discuss your options further with you. We'll arrange a get-together appointment."

"But I don't—"

He laughed, making her skin tingle. "Not a counselling appointment, Lucy. You seem to have your life on-track already. I just meant some general brainstorming on career choices."

Someone tapped on the door.

"Five minutes!" he called out. Then he said to Lucy, "For now, we'll concentrate on the set design. Welcome aboard. Can you be here well before school on Thursday?"

"Yes."

"By seven-thirty? We'll make it a breakfast meeting. It'll be a one-off. The rest of the design will double-deck with the drama classes."

"No problems."

Have to catch an early train.

They smiled at one another, and he took her hand briefly.

Mister Herron was anything but touchy-feelie, but unlike most of the teachers, he didn't shy away from the occasional contact. His hand was warm, and Lucy had to force herself not to cling.

"Tomorrow, Lucy," he said, and it sounded like a promise.

Lucy let herself out of the office. She didn't look at the little alcove where August's counselling students waited, but she knew the screen was drawn. She called softly, "Mister Herron is free now. I'm sure he'll know how to help you."

A choked sob acknowledged her.

Poor you, whoever you are.

She hurried off, with Mister Herron's voice ringing in her memory.

You seem to have your life on-track already. Tomorrow, Lucy.

Lucy caught the six-thirty train on Thursday morning and arrived at the office door by twenty-past. Nelis Winter, Sierra Sinclair, and Toshi Kahn were there. A couple of minutes later, an odd, eager new boy, whose name was Xavier Partridge but whom everyone called Bird Boy, arrived with Mister Herron. They were carrying baskets of something that smelled good.

Lucy realised, with a sinking feeling, that they were *all* here for the breakfast meeting.

So much for the two of us working one-on-one. Maybe I should have said Yes to Ms Shackleton . . . I could have been Queen of the May.

She put the thought away.

Working alongside August Herron on a challenging pro-ject was wonderful anyway, even with all those others. It gave her a secret buzz that lasted right up to the end of the school year, but she never forgot she might have been *Queen of the May*.

CHAPTER TWO: HERE WE GO AGAIN

Lucy Tan, 2012, Diversity High

Lucy was still in love with August Herron when she started Year Twelve. She'd thought not seeing him for six weeks over the summer might have desensitised her, but her first sight of his familiar and beloved form in the PD classroom brought a bright rush of delight.

Here we go again.

The thought wasn't painful. Having a secret love brought joy to her life.

I love him! He's lovely to everyone, but I'm the one who gets to love him.

"This term we're going to stretch ourselves and try some new techniques. You'll be surprised at what you can achieve if you're prepared to give it a go," he said.

Lucy felt he was speaking directly to her. This was the year they were going to have discussions about her future.

"Now is the time to visualise what you want out of life. By the end of this year, most of you will officially be adults, with access to all kinds of new experiences."

It was testimony to how well-liked August was that no one made crude suggestions about what some of those experiences might be.

"Just because you *may*, doesn't mean you *must*, or even *should* partake in everything on offer. Choose your experience wisely. My best advice to you is to *know yourselves*. Know your moral compass. Think *now* about the person you want to be for the next sixty or so years, the kind of experiences you'll remember with a smile, and the kind you might regret later."

That brought a few murmurs, and Nelis Winter came out of her habitual silence to say, "Have you any experiences to regret, Mister Herron?"

"A very few . . . and no, I'm not going to tell you. What saved me is the advice I just handed on to you. It is thanks to my wise old grandad that I'm the wonderfully *together* person you see before you." He bowed with a pantomime flourish.

General laughter.

He spread his arms as if to embrace them all. "Close your eyes and visualise a scene from your future. Then spend some time thinking about how to make it happen, or to prevent it from happening. If there are obstacles, come up with creative ways to solve them. We're not going to share the results of these exercises. I won't ask, and I hope none of you will press anyone else to tell. If anything comes up that troubles you, you know where my office is, and you all have the *app app*."

Lucy closed her eyes.

We're leaning over a design tablet, brainstorming together. You lean over and kiss me . . .

Don't be silly. He's your teacher.

Yes, but when I leave school . . . Maybe . . .

When you leave school, you'll never see him again.

Eyes still closed, she frowned. It was so unfair. As a student, she could spend hours in his company, knowing he would *never* overstep the boundaries. Once she left school, the boundaries dissolved, but then she'd never be in his company.

Obstacle. Right. Obviously, I need to train as a teacher.

She knew it couldn't work. It would take time to get her degree, and then she could be sent to any school in the country . . .

But I'd be moving in the same circles. I can legitimately keep in touch. I can mention teaching when we have those career meetings . . .

After the *Queen of the May* affair, she was resigned rather than disappointed to find out that at least half her visual arts class had career counselling appointments with Mister Herron. She was tempted to manufacture a personal problem and use the appointment app to schedule a counselling session.

After hearing sobs from the small waiting alcove, she knew she could never do it. What could she say?

I'm in love with my visual arts teacher . . .

She laughed at herself.

It's not a problem. It's something wonderful.

Under his friendly gaze, she felt she was slowly coming into bloom.

She knew she wasn't special to him . . . or no more than his other students were special. But still . . .

She hugged her truth in her heart.

He's special to me. I love him.

And then, not long before she turned eighteen, August Herron invited her to his office for a meeting and everything changed.

Chapter Three: The Proposition

Lucy Tan, 2012, Diversity High

The appointment was on Saturday. No one else was present when she got to the school, except for the groundsman, Mister Miller, who was pruning the ornamental hawthorn in the grounds.

Why? Why prune a tree when it's in flower?

"Good morning, Mister Miller."

He gave her a shy nod and a little smile. "Good morning, miss."

She almost laughed, but of course, he wouldn't know her name.

"I'm Lucy," she said.

She was going to see August Herron! The thought sent tingles of delight along her limbs, although she knew from experience that he'd doubtless invited others.

"Lucy . . . full of light," the man said, putting down the armful of flowering boughs.

Is he quoting poetry?

She mentally smacked her fingers. Who was she to assume a groundsman had no interest in poetry or plays or whatever he was riffing on?

Being a groundsman isn't what he is. It's what he does.

The light shone on his dark red hair. He had a smudge of paint on the thumb that operated the secateurs.

"It's a lovely tree," she said.

"Thorny." He tapped a small scratch on his wrist and then

added, "The flowers make it worthwhile, and then it gives us berries."

"That's life," she said.

"Oh, believe it!" he responded.

She went around to the back entry and then tapped for admission.

Where is everyone? Am I the first one here?

She listened for the tap of heels on the floor as Mister Crowther, the school secretary, came to unlock. Silence.

The door opened, apparently by itself.

Lucy raised her eyebrows. Of course, she knew Mister Herron could do that sort of thing, but he was generally circumspect about it.

She stepped in, and the door closed quietly behind her.

From that entrance, August Herron's office was three doors down the corridor. She raised her hand to tap.

The door opened.

August wasn't behind his desk. He was sitting in an armchair, relaxed and gorgeous in what looked to Lucy like a nineteenth-century costume of trousers, boots and a collarless shirt with a waistcoat. She almost shied back because it was just about the last thing she expected.

He smiled at her across the small table positioned beside his chair. "Hello, Lucy. I'm glad you could make it."

"Did you think I wouldn't?"

"No. I thought you would."

"Why?"

"Reliability and curiosity are two of your defining characteristics."

What about a healthy dose of unrequited love? She put that last in mental air quotes.

"Choose a mug and sit down," he said, waving his hand to a matching chair.

Lucy walked over to the wall of mugs and cups and examined them. Then she glanced over her shoulder. "Mister

Herron, is this some kind of test? Like those inkblot tests?"

He laughed. "I use my collection for cues to personality and preferences sometimes, but today I'm just offering you a cup of tea or coffee. By the way, you can call me August, or Augie, today, if you like, since this isn't official school business."

"It's not?"

"No. This is a meeting between two people. It happens to take place in a school, but it's not school business. I'm sorry if I gave you the impression it was."

Lucy selected a green cup in eggshell porcelain, decorated with sprays of pink and white blossom that reminded her of Mister Miller and the hawthorn tree. It was delightful, and so much prettier than the other cups.

He should have more lovely ones.

As she turned away from the selection, she noticed a set of women's clothing on a wooden hanger hooked into the picture rail.

Her stomach twinged with excitement, and her heartbeat tripped.

August waited until she was settled in the armchair before he picked up the pot that steamed on the table. He must have got it while she was choosing a cup.

Nonsense. He conjured that. This really isn't school business. He's not your teacher today.

"Tea? Coffee?"

"Tea, please. What's this all about?"

He poured tea into her cup and his own, which was white, clunky and decorated with a large capital D.

He should have a nicer one.

And, why D? His initials are AH.

AH, a softly exhaled sigh. An exclamation of inspiration.

She wondered what he'd have done if she'd asked for coffee.

He nodded towards a covered plate, which had also

materialised while she examined the china. "Sandwiches, if you want something to eat."

Lucy lifted the cover. The bread looked home-made.

"What's this about, Mister — August?"

He leaned forward and took a sandwich. "Nothing sinister, I promise you."

"No? Then why —" She tried to come up with a word that wasn't *secrecy*.

He watched her and asked, "Would you feel more comfortable if I call Mister Miller to join us? I think he's still out in the grounds. Ms Shackleton lives just down the street, if you want some female company. We could go to a café, but that might be a little awkward."

Oh my yes, that would be very awkward. We'd end up on Guest-Who *in no time.*

"It's fine." She picked up a sandwich. It was a solid rectangle, and when she bit off a crust, it crunched.

"Do you remember a conversation we had when I asked you to join the design team for *Queen of the May*?"

She nodded, not reminding him that he'd phrased it in a different way back then.

"I said then that we'd discuss your future at some point."

"I remember." She added deliberately, "It's something you did with almost everyone in our year."

"Just about," he agreed, unruffled. He leaned forward again, and she caught the fresh scent of bean flowers.

Her stomach clenched.

"Those group sessions were the preliminary rounds, if you like. Now it's time for the talk I really had in mind. And before you ask, I don't plan to have this one with your classmates. Not yet, at any rate."

She put down the sandwich.

"No good?" he asked.

"I'll eat it when you tell me what's going on." She smiled

faintly. "This is the point where I should tell you I know self-defence. My cousin Dequan taught me how to fell an ill-intentioned person with one sweep of my leg and an elbow in the soft parts."

August gave his delightful smile. "I remember a lad named Dequan . . . but he's . . ."

"Tall, blond surfer dude," she said equably. "My uncle married a woman whose family came from Holland. I call her *Tante Lotte.* She's fun. Hence, Dequan Qin's eyes do not disappear when he laughs."

"I'm glad your cousin taught you to take care of yourself, but I assure you there's *no harm* here. I mean, I'm not being wilfully mysterious or even wilfully creepy."

You so are.

"I invited you here because I have a proposal for you to consider."

Her stomach clenched again, and she looked at him mutely.

"It's for a position . . . a job, if you like . . . starting in late December. I've got to know all you seniors pretty well over the years, and I think you especially would be well-suited to this kind of work. If you like the idea, of course, and if you have no set plans for the next few months."

"What kind of work?"

"You could say it's work a bit like mine. Only you don't need formal qualifications. You get them on the job. You'd be working with me, initially."

"Set design?"

"Project design, broadly, but dealing directly with clients. Mentoring. Facilitating. Being approachable, but knowing where the line is drawn. I believe you'd be good at it, and I think you'd find it interesting."

"What's the catch?" At seventeen, Lucy had enough of her parents' worldliness to look every gift horse in the mouth and to count its teeth. Her heart revved into a glad gallop. She discovered she didn't care how many teeth this gift horse had.

August said, "No catch, Lucy. Unless you call living on an isolated island with no mod cons for weeks on end a catch."

Living with you? Working with you?

She breathed in deeply, catching the faint sweet scent of him again.

"Reality TV? Scientific research?" She tried to sound cynical as she lifted the cup to sip her tea. It was a beautiful cup, and she curved her fingers around its cheeks.

"Nothing like that. At least — it *is* like a reality TV set-up in a way, but there are no scripts, no cameras, and no viewers . . . ever."

"I don't get it."

"I'm explaining this badly, but it's all a bit fluid so far. We know how it will work in theory. We have yet to see *if* it will work in practice."

"Who is *we?*"

He picked up a sheaf of papers and pushed one across the table. It was a sketch map, with a few points marked in ink.

She put down her cup, untasted.

"This is Ferris Island. It's off the coast some considerable distance. There's no commercial access, and no permanent buildings. If you decide to come to the island, you'll be sailing there and back on *Robinson Crusoe*." He tapped a brochure showing a sailing ship. "She's a replica, made using traditional materials and craft. She belongs to the company whose project this is."

"Which company is this?"

He lifted a folder and flipped it over to land in her lap. "The Vouch-Safe company, which purchased Ferris when it came up for sale. Vouch-Safe is run by a group of —"

Lucy broke in, "I know about Vouch-Safe. My grandmother Qin bought a voucher for Mum and Dad's anniversary."

"Where did they go?"

Lucy shrugged. "Gran thought it would be fun to send Mum and Dad off to an unidentified destination in a situation they couldn't control. They're both control freaks. She's rather wicked, but I think she meant well this time. I'm sure she'd have loved it in her hippy flower child period."

He nodded, eyes crinkling in amusement. "One person's dream is someone else's nightmare."

"She didn't bank on them just sticking the voucher in the all-sorts drawer and forgetting about it."

"They could probably redeem it for cash."

"Oh no, Dequan found it when he was looking for a corkscrew during our New Year's Eve party, and they said he could have it. I intend to wring every scrap of information I can out of him." She picked up the tea again and sipped it and then smiled. "You got this tea from the alplands."

"Can't put anything past you, Lucy."

"Not much," she agreed. She added, "Gran Qin drinks it."

"She's fay?"

"That depends on what you mean. The Chinese blood from both sides of our family is human. It goes back to the gold rush. Dequan and I are descended from families who came out for the mining and found more profitable ways to live. Since they acquired bricks and mortar rather than portable gold, they stayed on and married one another. Gran Qin looks like an older version of me, but she has just enough *other* blood to open the gateways. She says she's almost a quarterling. Does that make sense to you?"

"Perfect sense. It means none of her grandparents is full fay, but possibly one was a halfling and another was a quarterling."

"I should ask her, but she's quite old, and Mum isn't open to that kind of family research. I can't open the gates, unfortunately. I can't see them. Not even a glimmer. I don't think Mum even wants to see them. She wasn't pleased when Gran took me *over there*." She looked at him directly. "You're an elf."

"I'm impressed."

"No need to be. Gran said you probably were. She's the reason I came to Diversity in the first place. I think she visualised a kind of Hogwarts situation."

"Then I imagine she was disappointed on Grandparents' Day," he said gravely.

"Hm. Not a robe or a wand in sight, but she did spot an elf."

"Vouch-Safe has a number of fay on its books, but this new venture — we call it the Eighteen Hundreds Squad Camp, but that's just temporary — is mainly for humans who want, or need, a break from modern life."

He told her about the job in more detail, and Lucy listened with attention, drinking tea and eating sandwiches, and occasionally asking a question.

After an hour, he said, "I suggest you take these papers home and give them a look over. If you'd like the summer job, let me know before the end of November, and then get your parents to sign the permissions."

"Summer job?" She felt a pang of disappointment. She'd assumed he was offering a proper full-time job.

"We're sailing over for a couple of weeks to set things up on the island. It will become self-sufficient in time, but we need supplies to start with. If you decide to stay on past that first set-up period, you'll be acting as paid companion and camp counsellor, as I said. If you enjoy the work, and if you prove suitable, then it can be an ongoing job. It wouldn't necessarily preclude you from taking on other work or study, but you would need to plan your schedule. Working remotely from the island won't be possible."

"No internet."

"No internet. No computers. No electricity. No coffee

19

shops. After the set-up period, no modern paper, even. If you find it's not to your taste, then you can collect your pay and a reference at the end of summer, and head off to university or into the job market or do some of the things we discussed before."

She nodded, remembering those discussions, taken with at least one other student present. He'd been sounding them out.

Is this allowed? Does the school know what he's up to?

August said, "I should warn you there are strict codes of behaviour for both campers *and* companions. I'll make sure you get a code of conduct list before you sign your contract. That, by the way, can be for just the summer, or for however many months you choose."

"Do you know what the rules are?"

"I do. In fact, I helped to formulate them."

"And you'll be bound by them?"

"Yes. They're strict, but not unreasonable. They're all made with a view to minimising stress and problems and maximising the autonomy and integrity of the camp."

"Then I'm in. Sign me up for six months." Lucy pushed the papers back across the table.

He smiled and lifted his winged brows. "Just like that, Lucy Tan?"

"Just like that, August Herron."

"Are you sure your parents will sign the permissions?"

Not a snowball's hope in hell. "They won't need to. I'll be eighteen well before then."

"You should still show them . . . They can check us out."

"No need." She might have added, *and I want to be near you. I like you. I trust you. I love you.*

She didn't. Instead, she jabbed her thumb towards the clothing hanging from the picture rail. "Is that for me to wear on the island?"

"Yes."

Luring me with clothes?

"Can I try it on now?"

"Certainly. Go down to the gym and change there."

She said, daringly, "You could conjure them on for me. I wouldn't tell."

"I could, but I won't, so there will be nothing to tell. Off you go before I change my mind."

"About conjuring?"

"No. About offering you the job."

He was smiling, but there was a slight edge to his voice. He meant it. She went.

The clothing fitted perfectly. She gazed at herself in the mirror of the girls' change room, at the high-waisted brown skirt, made in lined wool so soft it was more like worn cord, a linen blouse, and an apron with deep pockets. There was a loose jacket with a generous pleat in the back, knee-high stockings that tied below the knee, and soft leather boots.

Lucy lifted her hair and piled it into a bun.

She looked quaintly old-fashioned and very grown-up.

Not like a schoolgirl at all.

Her heart sang.

PART TWO: ISLAND

CHAPTER FOUR: JACK

August Herron, 2020, Diversity High

As an elf whose family had *lived human* for decades, Augie Herron was used to the vagaries of humans. As a school counsellor and visual arts teacher at Diversity High, whose motto was along the lines of *We Welcome Alternatives,* he was accustomed to teenagers who ranged from full human to the occasional full fay and everything in between. He acted as sponsor for young fay who wanted to learn to *pass as human,* and sometimes that was the hardest part of his life. He had to coach and counsel them, but he also had to know when to stand back and let them get into pickles and get themselves out.

He'd stood back too far, once, and ended up with a trembling young man babbling in his arms about how he'd *never meant it* and *I love her* and *how will she ever forgive me?* The *she* was an odd seventeen-year-old named Nelis Winter, whom young Xavier Partridge had assumed had *enough years* as well as the urgent desire to be his lover.

Augie had comforted the young man as well as he could, and he assured him no harm was done. He went to the unprecedented lengths of involving another student to give Nelis sanctuary and support. Inevitably, Lucy Tan was his choice for this intervention.

Lucy was always his choice, and she'd never let him down in all these years.

That awkward incident was well in the past, and he'd been

much more careful since then.

All good. Augie often thought in human terms. It was difficult not to, since he dealt with them every day. *Teenagers! They're a whole other species . . .*

Today's challenge had nothing to do with teenagers. It had to do with Jack Miller, the school groundsman.

Jack and Augie had worked at the same campus for years, but school demographics meant they spent little time together. Augie took his morning tea and lunch in the staffroom, in his office or occasionally while wandering around the grounds with his elf senses alert for trouble.

Jack, a tall man with pale skin, a thatch of dark red hair and grey eyes, ate in the greenhouse, the potting shed or down among the vegetables the agricultural students grew. He was in his late forties, Augie thought, and . . . he struggled to find the right term. *Bashful? Shy? Withdrawn?* None quite fitted. Neither did *simple, challenged* or even *quiet.* Jack wasn't surly or uncouth. He just kept to himself. He went about his jobs calmly and efficiently, and he nodded to any student who murmured *Good morning, Mister Miller,* in passing. Augie liked him, but he barely knew him.

Nodding terms just about covered the extent of their acquaintanceship. Occasionally, it was *smiling terms.* Definitely *blushing terms,* the first time Augie came to school early to catch up on some work and found Jack singing among the parsnips.

He had a fine tenor voice, but it was the song that astonished Augie. He knew that song, but he was surprised that Jack did. It was a fay song, and he'd never before heard it on *this* side of the gates.

"*The Water Carol,*" he observed, into the embarrassed silence.

Jack blushed.

Today's encounter was Jack's idea. Three times a day, Augie checked the app his students used to make appointments.

The app app, they called it.

Sometimes, it was a first name or a full name, or just a sad little *Please help me, Mister Herron. I've stuffed up.* He always responded right away with *Come to my office* or *Let me know where and when you'd like us to meet.* Today, the appointment was requested by *J. Miller. After school.*

Miller was a common name, and in the context of Diversity High, the J could have stood for Jonquil, Jai or January. Augie acknowledged the note with a friendly, *I'll be in the office from half-past three until five.*

At three-thirty-five, he heard a tap on the door.

"Come in." He looked up with his professionally friendly smile, expecting to see Jonquil, Jai or January sidle in. His money was on January, whose parents were halfway through a messy divorce.

When the tall groundsman stepped in and hesitated by the visitor's chair, Augie couldn't suppress a slight lift of his eyebrows.

"Good afternoon, Mister Miller."

The man nodded and asked, "Mind if I get myself a cup of tea, Master Herron?"

Master, eh? First card on the table. This is going to be interesting.

Augie gestured to the kettle and tea things by his sink. "Kettle just boiled."

He watched as Jack Miller made his tea and sat down. He'd chosen a dainty china mug with a pattern of soft pink roses and herons. Augie had an impressive collection of mugs and cups. His students often gave them to him as parting gifts when they left the school. The rose and heron mug had been an anonymous present, but he was sure it was from Lucy Tan. The heron obviously represented him, but why a pink rose? He could ask an expert, but after what he thought of as *the punch with the punch affair,* he was a little nervous about the possible answer.

Reliable Lucy. Lovely Lucy. Sensible Lucy.

"Guess you're surprised to see me, Master Herron," Jack said, setting his tea down on a cork coaster.

"Call me *August* if you like. Or *Augie.*"

"Okay. Funny how August or June or May or even April sound fine for names but January . . . that's my cousin's girl . . . just sounds odd."

Augie sipped his coffee and waited. His daughters were named Gianetta and Bethlehem. Could those be considered odd? Unlike some orders of the fay, the elves had eclectic naming practices.

Nothing more was forthcoming, so he said, "Have you come to see me about January? I know she's having a rough time."

Jack grimaced. "Yes, poor kid. I'd like to have words with Grant on account of that. Not that I think he and his missus should stay together if they're not happy, but —" He gestured his distaste. "It's not about Janny, anyway. I need your help."

He looked up and met Augie's gaze squarely. "It's about my son."

"I don't think I know him. Is he here at school?"

Jack shook his head. "He can't . . . *pass.*"

Oh. Cards even more clearly on the table.

Augie smiled. "You're fay?"

Braesider? He has the height for it, and he might be glamouring his eyes.

Jack snorted with apparent amusement. "Not so as you'd notice. My great-grandfather was a leprechaun man, but aside from old Patsy Shillelagh's green blood, I'm human. You're not, though. Pixie man?"

"No, I'm an elf."

"Right. I only thought pixie because of the fix-its, on account of what you do."

Augie relaxed. If Jack knew that much, the conversation should be easier. "Pure elf, as far as I know. My family *lives human,* but we have some fairly distant relatives *over there,* so we visit with our girls. How may I help you?"

"It's about my boy. Paris. He's . . . he's the best son a man ever had. I always hoped he might come and spend time with me so we could do all the stuff dads do with their kids, but I brought him over once, and he couldn't hack the atmosphere." He shrugged. "Fee warned me, but I thought it was just — you know — tradition. Even superstition. Seems it's not. Paris wanted to come, so it wasn't psychological."

"Fee's his mother?"

"Yes. And my love. Her folk hardly ever marry, and I live *over here.* I see her as often as I can. We're a family."

"How do you get there?" Augie asked. It required more fay blood than Jack had to open the gateways between the human and fay realms.

"I use the gateway on the north shore . . . through the courtyard of a terrace house. Mistress Joan lets me through. It started when Great Aunt Nora, that's Grandad Miller's sister, was alive. She *lived human,* the way you do, and she used to go through to see her dad and her brothers at Blarney Edge. They could just about *pass,* but they didn't want to. She said if I ever wanted to go through without her, I could go to the north shore gate and ask one of the Treadwells . . . it was Mistress Dara or Master Arthur in those days . . . to let me through. So I did."

He seemed to think that explained it. Augie supposed it did. He waited.

"I used to go through and hang out with the leppy cousins. They laughed at me for being a *cream man,* but it was all in fun. I even picked myself a leppy last name, though I put it in the middle. I took *Blarney.* It isn't official, but it's good to have that link back to the past." He smiled suddenly. "Paris chose the same one without me prompting him. Not that he needed to. He's what — one-sixteenth? Barely leppy at all, but the green-bloods at Blarney Edge acknowledge him."

Of course, they do. Leprechauns seem to know if a gossoon so much as glanced at your great-great-great-great granny on a dark night back in the eighteen-hundreds. If he took her to the shamrock banks . . . well!

Augie waited patiently. At least this story made a change from dealing with teenage traumas.

"I got along better with those gossoon cousins than with my own kind. I went out with a few girls from school or work, but it never lasted. I remembered the leppy boys and their straight-to-it courtships, so I went looking *over there*. I hoped I might get picked by a colleen . . . how's that for arrogance?"

August gave the required *what can I say?* gesture. Leprechaun colleens could have their pick of the fay men. Some of them settled with humans, but those would be actively looking *over here*.

Jack said, "No such luck. Just as well, considering how big I am and how small they are. The tree maids steered clear of me, too. Same reason, I guess. I got glowered at by a pixie man for asking a miss to dance and . . . laughed at by a couple of pisky minxes for not recognising their earring status . . . let's just say I ended up at the falls as a default. You know what I mean."

"I do."

"I thought if I got *educated,* then I mightn't be so awkward with girls at home."

Augie nodded. "I got my own education at the falls."

"You *did*?"

"Oh, yes. My family *lives human*, but my uncle suggested I should learn what went where from an expert before I started courting and shamed myself and my line." He smiled at the old-fashioned term. Humans barely used it anymore. The fay still did. "There's no one more expert than the waterfolk and no one kinder to an awkward young man than a water maid . . . or a lad, come to that."

Jack took a swallow of his tea, and he grimaced. "I wouldn't know about lads. I'm strictly a one-way street. Look here. This is going to be a bit of a long story. Is that okay?"

August made an expansive gesture. "Yes, just tell it in your own way."

Jack nodded, and then he began.

CHAPTER FIVE: LOVE BY THE FALLS

August Herron, 2020, Diversity High

Jack said, "I went to the falls and stood there gawping at all those naked lovelies. I wasn't sure if I had to make the approach or if they would."

"They do," August said.

"One certainly did. Next thing you know, a small warm cannonball hit me, and I fell in the pool. Clothes gone, gasping for air, thrashing about . . . and then *she* said, *You like it in water, lad? If not, I have a fine braeside plaid to warm your bum.*"

He gave a rueful smile. "I opted for the plaid. Her name is Fee, and I found out she specialised in knocking men into the pool. She still does it."

"So you got educated," Augie murmured.

"Did I what! It was—I'd never felt so . . ." He paused, frowning over the word. "Valued," he said finally. "When we'd done it, she gave me this huge smile and said she thought I was lovely and she wanted to have me again. Oh, and *again*, please. I found stamina I never knew I had, just because *she* wanted me. I spent two weeks with her there at the falls. Then I came home . . . and back to my senses. I realised I couldn't marry her and live there. I'm not waterfolk, and that life's not possible for humans. Not in the long term. Our skin won't take all that submersion. I'd lost my job through being AWOL, but there was a vacancy here at Diversity, and I applied. I thought the long holidays would give me time to be with Fee if she still wanted me. She did. Still does. And I've worked here ever since."

He smiled again and seemed to relax. "I spend a few days or a few weeks with Fee and our boy as often as I can. It's still magic. She still shoves me in the pool and jumps on me. She still loves and wants me, and she still says, *Again!* Then, when I have to come home for work, she just gives me an extra big kiss and hugs me. Then she gives her lovely smile and says, *Most darling Jack, I'll see you soon.* And our boy Paris gives me a hug and says, *Till then, my father. Don't forget it's a shining world.* I used to tell him that when he was a tiddler. He's tall like me. Red-haired, too. I guess he couldn't avoid that, since Fee's a redhead."

Augie nodded encouragingly. It was an odd story, but it explained quite a lot about Jack.

He's a romantic. He loves his family, and he misses them, but he wouldn't be half so happy with a full-time suburban wife who worries about her waistline and reminds him about the job jar.

He didn't know Fee personally, but he was sure she was every bit as beautiful, energetic and loving at forty-whatever as she'd been at twenty. Waterfolk loved life until one day they didn't . . . and then they went down to the sea to *feel the waves.* He didn't know the details, but he knew it was a fine system, for them.

Jack finished his tea and set down the mug. "Fee would like this pattern," he said, gesturing to the roses and birds. "She had a Cornfellow creamware set with waterlilies on it. Came as a surprise to me. Never would have expected waterfolk to brew tea until she gave me some after our second session on the blanket."

August wouldn't have expected it, either. Waterfolk typically didn't bother with possessions.

"She has another set she uses now," Jack said.

Augie said gently, "That's quite a story, Jack. But I'm not clear on why you came to see me. If you wanted to talk about *over there* and your family, you could have come to have a

31

yarn over a beer at the pub or dropped in after school, unofficially. I've been working here for years, so why come to me now?"

"I've been here longer than you, but most people don't notice the groundsman. I keep to myself here. My heart's *over there.*"

That should have sounded odd from the tall man in overalls and a flannelette shirt and unexpectedly beautiful grey eyes, but it didn't.

"So?" Augie spent a lot of his time gently drawing out distressed, resentful or miserable teenagers, but Jack was an adult, so he didn't feel it appropriate to coax out confidences.

Jack looked up, and Augie saw hope in his eyes.

What does he want? Whatever is he asking?

"Jack . . ."

Jack took an audible breath and made his request.

Augie prided himself on never seeming taken aback, or shocked . . . but this time, he really couldn't help it.

"I don't think—"

"I *wish* you could see your way to helping me, Master Herron," Jack said clearly.

CHAPTER SIX: EIGHT YEARS ON

Cherie and Adam Tan, 2020, Sydney

Eight years after signing her first six-month contract, Lucy Tan still worked for Vouch-Safe. She still regularly boarded the ship *Robinson Crusoe* to sail to Ferris Island with the latest batch of campers. She said she loved her job.

Lucy's parents didn't love her job. They weren't even sure what it was. Cherie and Adam Tan were a corporate couple who had done their best to give Lucy every opportunity in life. It wasn't their fault Lucy had *dropped out* – their term – to work for the Vouch-Safe company. Cherie blamed August Herron, whose influence she had distrusted ever since her mother, Juliana, mentioned his order.

Elves are not to be trusted.

Adam blamed Juliana directly.

Filling Lucy's head with all that woo-woo stuff.

They were right on both counts. Since they had ditched their traditional names of Chen and An, which meant *the morning* and *tranquil*, respectively, as soon as they could, they could hardly complain when Lucy staged her own gentle rebellion and refused to join the family firm.

Cherie and Adam wanted Lucy to go to university and join the corporate life as they had. They would have accepted it, though reluctantly, if she'd stuck with her suggested plan of teacher training.

Instead, she cut herself off from family, society and just about everything else for months on end.

They hoped she'd get it out of her system, settle with a suitable man and provide them with a grandchild. After eight years, Lucy still clearly loved her job and had no visible man, suitable or otherwise. The only people she seemed to socialise with were an odd young woman she'd known at school and her cousin, Dequan, who always looked to be having a secret joke at their expense.

That annoyed them.

As for that elf . . .

"He has some sort of hold over her," Cherie said fretfully to her mother.

Juliana Qin gave her an old-fashioned look. "Next, you'll be saying she's bringing up a nest of half-elf children out there on that island."

"For all I know, she could be."

"Darling Chen, you could always use that voucher I gave you to go and see."

Cherie snorted.

"Lucy loves you and An dearly, you know," Juliana said.

"Then why does she run away at every opportunity? Why won't she let us *in*?"

"I expect it's because you disagree with her on almost everything . . . Much easier to stay on nice terms if we don't live in one another's pockets, don't you see?"

"Mum, I—"Cherie looked sadly into her mother's dark, compassionate eyes, networked with wrinkles now.

"I know, darling Chen. So let's have tea next month, shall we? I'm sure we can achieve two hours of civility a month. Two hours is enough, because I love you dearly and I know you love me."

Chapter Seven: Punch with a Punch

Lucy Tan, 2012-13, Ferris Island

One night during the first week of what they now called Camp Ferris, Lucy revealed her love to August Herron.

She didn't intend to make her declaration in public, but one of the other companions offered round some celebratory punch as a trial batch for New Year's Eve. Lucy had just one small mug of the stuff. It tasted innocuous, but she discovered later that Patrice had added leprechaun poteen. She'd never touched the stuff since.

Nelis Winter, who had joined the group after a disastrous Leavers' Dinner at school, had already gone to bed in the tent they shared. She was still processing whatever trauma had led her to blow off the New Year's barbecue that should have ended her time at Diversity High.

Lucy stayed up. She wanted to let Nelis have some space, and she wasn't losing a moment of the time she spent with August. It had occurred to her, belatedly, that he wouldn't always be at Camp Ferris. When the school year began in January, he'd be back at Diversity High.

The companions-elect sat on blankets outside the tents, and one of the men conjured a long bolster to lean on so he could play his lute.

That led to some discussion about whether this action contravened the camp rules.

No personal belongings.

"It's a *blanket.* I got it from the stores, and the lute's from the stores as well," he defended himself.

"I thought it was yours, Colin? You had it at the marina," someone said.

"It *was* mine, until the moment I crossed the gangplank. Now it belongs to the island. I've donated it to the cause."

"Oh, in that case . . ."

There was general laughter, and someone started singing. *Beat of My Own Drum.*

A *frisson* ran down Lucy's back.

August joined the singer with the chorus line, and three others joined in.

Lucy remembered the lead part word for word, so she counted herself in and struck up the counter melody.

I'm the Queen of the May it seems . . .

The lutist fumbled a chord, and the song broke apart in good-natured laughter.

Another companion-elect, a thirty-something leprechaun colleen named Maeve, flicked her fingers and conjured a bed roll. "Come on and snuggle wid me, lover," she said, holding out an arm to Patrice.

They're not breaking the no fraternisation rule. They're an item already, Lucy told herself as the man, who seemed mostly human, shifted over to take up the invitation. He kissed Maeve with slow enjoyment.

"Want a back prop, darlin'?" the woman said, in her leprechaun lilt, smiling at Lucy when she'd surfaced.

"Yes, please!"

A rolled blanket landed near Lucy. She thanked Maeve and pushed it behind her. She took another sip of the punch, feeling warm, adult and accepted.

Bolstered by the blanket roll, the punch and Maeve's example, she turned to August. He was sitting cross-legged, watching the goings-on with an indulgent expression. She held out her arm as the colleen had done. "Like to cuddle, Augie?"

Her words fell into the conversation just a little too loudly.

A couple of the other companions glanced at her and then went back to sipping their drinks and roasting apples in the fire. The lutist settled into another tune.

In a perfectly natural voice, August said, "No, thanks, Lucy, I'm about to turn in." Then he raised his voice a little. "Patrice?"

Maeve's man lifted his mug in salute.

"What's in that punch?"

"Cold tea, apple juice, the last of the cider and a bit of plum brandy — oh, and a wee bit of stuff out of Maeve's brown bottle. Good, isn't it?"

"Very. But maybe we all should lay off for tonight."

"We'll have to. I just drank the last drop. I have to make some more for New Year, and it'll have to be sans cider," Patrice said placidly.

"Fair enough." August got to his feet. "Night, all."

There was a chorus of *goodnights*.

"Road rise to ye, elf man," the leprechaun woman said, kissing her fingers to him.

Lucy felt light-headed, flushed, over-warm from the fire, but chilled inside. She also felt as if a door had slammed abruptly in her face. She leaned on the blanket roll and closed her eyes. A tear forced its way through her clenched lids.

The talk swirled around her, and she was aware of other people gradually getting up to retire.

Someone touched her shoulder. She opened her eyes to see, through the blur, a dark-haired young woman with exotic features.

"You okay, Lucy?"

"Yes . . . um . . ."

"Asha," the woman reminded her. She slid down to sit cross-legged by Lucy. "That punch packs a punch," she said cheerfully. "I don't know anyone here. I was recruited with my girlfriend, but she changed her mind about the job . . . and me . . . on Christmas Eve. Great timing, huh."

"I'm sorry."

"So am I. I mean, what do you do with a sterling silver bangle engraved with A4Z4ever after the intended recipient has buggered off with a floozy from Freemantle?" She drew the inscription in the air with a casual finger. "I should at least have had the sense to put A4U . . . but that's TMI and not what I wanted to say right now."

Lucy braced herself for a big-sisterly lecture, but Asha said, "Some of these folk are obviously of the fay persuasion. I was surprised when that colleen conjured. I thought they couldn't, but maybe it's just *don't usually*. She's not the only one, either. The guy with the nice voice is an elf, and I reckon the lutist is a courtfolk halfling."

"So?"

"Alcohol doesn't affect fairies, *except* for leprechaun poteen. Half a glass gives them a mild buzz, but it would probably knock one of us out for three days straight. Wouldn't kill you, but it's not a good look. I suggest you enquire as to the antecedents of anything they offer you to drink unless it's plain tea. I imagine once we get into the routine, there won't be any strong drink here anyway unless someone starts up a still. Just until then . . . might be wise not to partake. I won't be drinking more of that punch."

"Okay. But surely no one —"

"No, my dear. Everyone here has been vetted for antisocial tendencies. I'm sure no one will knowingly slip you a mickey. They'd be out on their ear if they did, and trust me — no one is here who doesn't want to be. The fairies just won't consider the effect on the human constitution. You *are* human?"

Lucy was silent.

"Sorry, that's against the rules, too. Forget I asked." Asha got to her feet. "Don't worry, Lucy. No one will try to take advantage of you. I'm not cracking onto you. Celibacy is definitely on my cards for a few months, even if it wasn't camp policy. I need to put in some thought about why someone would bugger off with a Fremantle floozy when she could have had *me*." She delivered the last sentence with such dramatic irony that Lucy almost laughed. Why indeed? Asha was beautiful.

"You should get some sleep, Lucy. Your friend's already gone to bed."

August . . . Oh, she means Nelis.

Lucy nodded and agreed and headed off to her tent. Nelis was asleep, breathing quietly, so Lucy took off her boots and lay down as silently as she could, not wanting to wake her. Her head whirled.

She slept badly, and, as the warm buzz faded, the cold in her heart grew.

He turned me down. He didn't say Not just now. *He said* No, thank you.

She was still awake at five in the morning when a shadow fell across her tent.

"Who's there?" she called softly, wondering if Asha had come to check on her.

"It's me. August. Will you come for a walk with me? Nelis can come, too, of course."

Lucy was still dressed in the linen skirt and blouse that constituted the companions' summer clothing. She crawled out of the tent, and her heart did its usual glad skip to see August. He had his back to her.

"Nelis is still asleep," she said breathlessly.

He turned and looked at her gravely, and then smiled and tossed her an apple. "Sun's nearly up. If we go to the water caves, we might be lucky enough to see the reflections. Maeve and Patrice saw them yesterday."

Lucy pulled on her boots, and they set off through the predawn light. On the way, she ate her apple, which tasted almost but not quite the way apples usually did.

Must be an old variety they don't grow commercially.

When it became obvious that August wasn't going to mention the night before, she dropped the core in her pocket for composting later and broached the subject herself.

"I think that punch affected me last night. But I meant it when I offered you a . . . well, I meant it."

He said nothing.

She rushed on, "I know there's a no fraternisation rule unless there's an existing relationship, but we've known one another for six years. You know my real name, and Nelis's, and just about everything about us."

"I thought I knew you," he said.

He stopped and held out his hand, but not so she could take it. "Lucy, until last night, I had no idea you thought of me as anything more than your teacher and now your colleague."

She could have tossed it off, but she told him the truth. "I've loved you for two years."

"I'm sorry."

"No need to be *sorry*. I didn't set out to do it, and I haven't told anyone, ever. I don't regret it, and I'm not ashamed. You're just so—you. And now you're not my teacher anymore. I didn't mean to embarrass you."

"You surprised me."

"I don't see why. You can't be all that much older than I am. I mean, my father is nine years older—"

"It's not about age, and it isn't about you."

"It's not you. It's me?" She let the snap show in her voice.

"It's not even because I was your teacher and, until a few days ago, in a position of *loco parentis*."

"What then? You just don't fancy me? You don't like girls?"

"Lucy, my dear, I'm married to the love of my life. I have two children."

So that was that. He was unavailable for the most

persuasive and unassailable of reasons. His love belonged to somebody else.

Lucy rocked back on her heels. "But you—" She pulled herself together. "I see. You never mentioned that before. Never mentioned her. Them. Not once. Not in six years. Don't you think you might have just *once,* said, casually, *Gotta take this call. It's my wife?*"

"I never mention my family at school. Bizarre as it may sound to you, there's a good reason for that. Shall we keep walking?"

"Yes. All right." She felt like a popped balloon.

He went on, "My family is my life. The rest of it is work. The person you knew at school is a mask I put on."

"Mister Herron, the sexy, adorable teacher."

"That was never my intention. I strive to be friendly, approachable . . . helpful. I'm not my students' father, or uncle, or brother, or friend, but I have to project elements of all those. My role is teaching art techniques and helping students to avoid pitfalls and bringing them to find the best lives they can. That doesn't involve parading *my* life, because that's not the focus."

"So you don't really have a wise old grandad who gave you useful maxims."

"I do. I never tell lies to my students."

She clenched her hands. "You must think I'm a predictable idiot."

"I think you're my valued colleague in an interesting and exciting job. I hope you want to continue in that role."

"I do." She lifted her chin, and two tears slid down her cheeks. She didn't care if he noticed.

He didn't assure her she'd find a nice man to love or say she'd soon forget about him. He didn't hand her a handkerchief.

She loved him all the more for that.

They reached the water caves and stood in silence as the sun hoisted itself out of the sea and rays struck the still-dark water to reflect back in streaks of white gold.

"Beautiful," August murmured.

He didn't suggest the natural miracle put small hurts into perspective.

"Magical," Lucy said.

"Not in the fairy sense. Perhaps, in a wider sense."

"More things in Heaven and Earth."

The light show persisted for a few minutes and then vanished.

"We'd better go back now. I have to chop some wood for the cooking fire. How are you at stacking?"

"I don't know. Probably better than I am at chopping."

"We can take turn-about if you like. There are gloves in the stores."

She turned out to be good at stacking, neat and quick and able to judge the exact length needed to fill a gap in the pile. Nelis helped them, silent as usual. Lucy assumed she was still cut up about whatever had happened at the Leavers' Dinner. Maybe Nelis would tell her sometime, but she wasn't going to ask. Confidences were overrated.

That evening, Lucy went back early to the tent. This time, she undressed properly.

"Gloves or not, my hands are never going to be the same again," Nelis said out of the silence.

"I doubt if either of us will ever be the same again. Are you sorry you came?"

"I don't want to do this for the rest of my life, but it's just what I need for now. Thank you for inviting me. All this work is giving me back my self-respect."

"I'm glad you're here, too. It's good to have someone I know."

"You know Mister Herron."

There was no particular emphasis in her voice.

Lucy rolled over, feeling her long cotton nightgown catching around her knees.

"I thought I did," she said.

After that, she and August pretended their awkward conversation hadn't happened. And, luckily, he *rotated out* after the first influx of campers.

Back to his family. Back to his mask.

Lucy missed him fiercely, but by then she had her own niche on the island, and when her contract came up for renewal in May, she signed without a second thought.

As one of the original companions, and the one who had racked up the most shifts the regulations allowed, Lucy rolled her first contract's savings into shares in the company.

"But what do you *do*?" Cherie asked her on her first time home. She still resented Lucy's decision to leave home just before Christmas. "Not a word. Not a *word* for six months," she added fretfully.

"You knew I wouldn't be able to communicate from the island. And I do whatever's needed. I don't wait on people or organise them. I don't listen to their troubles, and I certainly don't sleep with them, if that's what's bothering you."

"That underhanded teacher of yours . . . He ought to be reported."

Lucy jumped on that before her mother said something they'd both regret.

"August has a wife and two children, and I'm sure he's never laid a finger where it shouldn't be in his life."

Cherie gave her a suspicious look.

Lucy drew in a deep breath. "I help the troubled to get untroubled, and the stressed to calm down. If they really can't do something for themselves, I demonstrate or explain until they can. I'm not their friend or their teacher. I'm a companion who knows the ropes."

"And that's all?"

"That's all. But it's the most satisfying job in the world."

CHAPTER EIGHT: CATCH AND RELEASE

Lucy Tan, 2013, Sydney

Lucy knew dating was going to be difficult, but she made up her mind her love for August Herron must not cripple her emotionally or sexually. He was hers to love, but *his* love belonged to his wife.

She gave some thought to Augie's advice to his flock at the beginning of Year Twelve. *Choose your experiences wisely so you can look back with a smile.*

She had her little car, which she'd bought with help from her parents in Year Twelve. Her cousin, Dequan, had *put her in the way of* it. Dequan always knew someone who knew someone, and he happened to know a young couple who had fallen pregnant with a third child and wanted to get a bigger car.

"It's in good nick, Lucy-Lou. Mechanically sound. You can take it for a test drive."

She took his advice and bought the car.

Dequan also *put her in the way* of a man who knew a woman who did dog walking at the local shelter.

"You can do your bit and get a doggie fix at the same time," he said when she bemoaned her inability to get a dog. Regulations meant she couldn't take it to camp.

Lucy thought, therefore, that Dequan might help with her latest need.

She went to his flat and let herself in, following her nose to the smell of a piquant tomato sauce he was making at the stove.

"Hey, Lucy-Lou. Want some?"

"Sure."

He poured the sauce over noodles, and they perched at the breakfast bar with brown bread and a bunch of grapes.

"So, what can I do you for?" he asked when their forks slowed.

"How do you know I want something?"

"You've got that predatory look in your eye."

She laughed. "Right. I want you to *put me in the way* of someone."

"Nothing illegal?"

"Give me a break."

"Immoral?"

"Hmm. Not from my perspective. Mum and Dad might frown."

"What would Gran Qin say?"

"She'd be astonished I've got to be this old without doing it."

"This sounds ominous. So — what?"

Lucy mopped up the last of the sauce and stuck the bread in her mouth.

"I want someone to take me to bed and teach me stuff."

Dequan choked.

"Not you, so don't even go there. I love you like a brother."

"Can't you —"

"I could, but I don't want to. I don't want to pick someone up in a pub, and I don't have time to go the whole getting-to-know-you route. I'll be back at work in a couple of weeks."

Dequan blew out his cheeks. "So what are your must-haves? What's negotiable? What are the deal-breakers?"

"Male. No one married, or exclusive. No one who's on the rebound, or is a bad way, emotionally. No one who can't hear the word *no*. No one who smells funny, or who smokes or takes weird substances. No one older than forty or younger than eighteen. I don't mind what nationality he is, or what he does for work, or if he's good-looking or not. I don't care what his religion is. I want to be able to look at him, after, and smile. I want to remember him, after, and smile. I don't want to worry about him after I go to work, and I don't want him to know my last name or my details. I don't want to know his, either."

"Is that it?" He sounded amused.

"More or less. Obviously, I want healthy and no nonsense about not wanting to use protection."

"Are you offering payment?"

"I'd rather not. I will, if necessary."

"And when do you want this person?"

"As soon as possible. I'm leaving in ten days."

Dequan considered, whistling through his teeth. Then he said, "Leave it with me. If I come up with someone, I'll message you. Just a tick." He pulled his phone out of his pocket, raised it and took her photo.

"Good idea," Lucy said. Then she added, "I don't want someone who'll mess me about. I'd rather do without."

"Don't worry. Anyone who tried to mess you about would have me to deal with. I love you like a sister."

They smiled at one another in perfect accord.

The message came from Dequan the next day.

Lucy-Lou — got a prospect for you. Name's Otto. He works in the music industry. Single, pragmatic, straight forward . . . and he's fay, and therefore inhospitable to STDs. Tell him no elfin babies or I'll have his nuts for my Waldorf. You can meet him at The Pear Tree *at three today. It's near that park we used to go to for the lantern festival. You'll see the pub if you look closely. Just order two hob ciders and ask for Otto.*

Lucy read the message three times and then tucked the

phone in her pocket.

She wondered what one wore for such an occasion and decided what she had on would do. The pink shirt lent warmth to her skin, and her jeans were old favourites.

Then she rethought the jeans. She might be sore, after, so she put on a full skirt and stuck an extra pair of knickers in her pocket.

Nightshirt? She wasn't planning to sleep with him.

Her parents were providentially at work, so she texted them to say she was out and might not be home for dinner.

Then she ran a comb through her dark hair and let herself out of the family home.

The Pear Tree was near the park, but she didn't recall seeing it before.

It lurked behind some trees, so she supposed it was an optical trick that hid it from casual passers-by.

She entered and looked about with interest. Two young women glanced at her, and one looked a little harder before turning away.

Maeve.

Not to worry, she was bound to see companions on R&R now and again. Lucy glanced about and spotted two men in kilts, and an elderly woman with delicately pointed ears and a great deal of silver jewellery.

Okay. It's a fairy pub.

She walked up to the counter, where a woman with milkmaid braids was polishing glasses.

"Two hob ciders, if you please, mistress."

Gran Qin had given her lessons on the proper mode of address for full fay ladies.

The woman frowned slightly. "Have you enough years?"

"I'm nearer to nineteen than to eighteen." Lucy produced her driver's licence.

"Very good. I had to ask."

"Fair enough." Lucy watched her pour cloudy gold liquid

into two heavy glasses. She presented her card, but the woman shook her head and indicated a sigh that said, *cash only.*

"The wards mess with the electronics," she said. She pushed the glasses over to Lucy. "Anything else, Lucy?"

Clever. You really did look at that licence.

Lucy grabbed her courage in both hands. "Is Otto here?"

"Yes, he came in a few minutes back. I'll call him." She turned, opened a pass door and called, "Otto! Your friend's here!" Then she turned to Lucy. "He's in the back bar. Go on through."

Heart thudding, Lucy carried the cider through the door. Beyond was a corridor, with a number of exits, all oddly labelled. One said, *Pear Tree Bar,* so she plumped for that one.

Inside, a massive publican was leaning on the bar, talking to a young man perched on a stool. He had his back to Lucy, but she saw he had short dark brown hair and casual clothes so unobtrusive they must be hand-made. She cleared her throat, and the man turned and smiled.

"Lucy! Glad you could make it." He indicated the barman. "This is Master Perry, the landlord. He's just leaving."

"Oh, is he indeed." The publican folded his arms across his massive chest.

"I believe so. Lucy and I have some business in Bedfordshire."

"Good afternoon to thee then." He smiled at Lucy. "Give the cider to Otto to carry, lass. The stairs are a mite steep." He took off his apron and went unhurriedly out into the corridor.

"Bedfordshire?" Lucy asked uncertainly.

The man indicated the corridor. "There's a sign out there. Let's sit here a while first, though."

He got off the stool and waved her over to a well-scrubbed table.

When they settled, he looked her over. "Okay, Lucy. Dequan told me what you wanted, and I agreed . . . subject to meeting you first and having this talk. I take it you're not Dequan's sister?"

"I'm not."

"But he was authorised to speak for you?"

Lucy leaned back. "Yes. I've known him all my life, and I trust him. We trust one another. I know where the bodies are buried, and vice versa."

"Good. You didn't consider him for your business?"

"No. I know him too well."

"And you wanted someone you don't know."

"Yes. I have work that makes the usual kind of relationships difficult because I'm away a lot."

"I see."

"So I want to know what I'll be saying *yes* to if and when I do get into a relationship." She took a sip of cider. It was strong and sweet, so she took a larger mouthful.

"Dutch courage?" Otto asked.

"Not really. Dequan said to order two of these and ask for you." She added, "There's another reason I wanted some experience. I have a medical scheduled before I leave, and I don't want the first person to touch me down there to be someone wearing gloves and holding something cold and metallic."

Otto laughed. "I see your point, Lucy. Is that your real name?"

"Yes. Is your real name Otto? You don't look German."

"It's my familiar name. It says Orlando on my papers. You're welcome to the rest of it, but Dequan said you preferred first names only."

"I do."

He drank some of the cider. "Is there anything else you want to ask me before we go upstairs? That's if you *do* want to go upstairs? If you've changed your mind, we'll say good-bye."

Lucy considered. "Did Dequan tell you my checklist?"

"He did. Very particular, aren't you? And before you ask, *yes*, he informed me of my role in a future Waldorf salad if I neglect to *hold*. He also said you were willing to pay me, but I think that would be peculiar. I've had lovers in the past, but no one currently. I've never paid or been paid. I'm happy to oblige you."

Lucy swallowed more cider.

"That's probably enough if you want to remember the experience," Otto said.

She sipped again and handed him the half-empty glass. "Bring it upstairs. In case I need to forget in a hurry."

Otto got to his feet and picked up his own glass. He gestured to the door. "Go through there and into the door that says *Bedfordshire*. Up the stairs, there are some rooms. Open the first door and go on in. I'll be with you in a couple of minutes."

Lucy got up obediently and did as he instructed.

The room was plain but pretty, with cheerful print curtains and a double bed covered with a matching spread. A small bathroom led off to one side, and a wide chair dominated the space by the bed.

A guitar case and a small holdall leaned against the wall.

Lucy took off her shoes and put her bag on the chair. After a few seconds, she stripped off and got into the bed. The sheets were clean and cool. She thought they were linen.

Someone tapped on the door. "Lucy?"

"In here."

He came in, still holding the cider, which he set on a small table.

"This is a nice room," Lucy ventured.

"It is, and before you start wondering, this is a perfectly normal motel room. It's not rented by the hour, and this place is not a brothel. I have the use of it while I'm in town, in exchange for playing some sets in the evenings."

She relaxed.

"Your friend left it to me to pick the venue, and I thought this would be more comfortable than the back of a car and less compromising than my flat, which is a good way out. Wherever you live would also be compromising. I come here sometimes, but don't let that trouble you. If you ever come into the pub and see me, you can pretend you didn't, or you can smile and say hello. I won't approach you, but neither will I snub you. And I will never speak of this to anyone, including Dequan. You are welcome to tell him as much or as little as you choose, but *I* won't."

Lucy said, "I'm impressed. You've thought of everything."

"Just about. Anything else?"

She shook her head.

He raised a hand, and his clothing vanished, landing in a pile on the chair. He stood for a moment, slender and well-muscled, and then turned back the covers and got into bed beside her.

"I don't know what I'll do. How I'll react, I mean," Lucy said.

"Want a safe word?"

"*No* and *wait*?"

"Fine."

He held out an arm. "Roll up against me."

She complied. His skin smelled of summer at the beach. After a bit of thought, she identified it as a yellow acacia tree that grew near the sea.

"Relax," he said.

"I don't relax at the dentist, either."

"The —"

She laughed, realising he'd probably never needed to go.

"That's better." He pulled her closer, rolled in, and kissed her brow. "Okay?"

"Mm. You smell nice."

He nuzzled her neck. "Ticklish?"

"No."

He kissed her cheeks and then her lips and then put his hand on her chest.

"Don't be scared. Is there someone you wish was here instead of me?"

She thought of Augie. She loved him, but she would never go to bed with him. He had a wife.

"No. I'm happy for it to be you."

"And are you sure you want your first time with a stranger?"

"I told you — no gloves or — "

He rolled her over on top of him, and she felt something probing between her legs.

She caught her breath, but the feeling stopped.

"Not ready yet. I'm going to fix that. Just keep your legs relaxed."

He rolled her off and kissed down her breastbone to her belly. Lucy closed her eyes as his lips brushed between her legs. His hands urged her legs apart, and he kissed and licked until she was squirming.

"I'll try a finger now," he murmured.

A finger entered her cautiously, and she gasped. Another joined it, and a third.

"Ah-ah . . ." She writhed.

"Does that hurt?"

It did, but she was desperate for what she knew would come.

"Please . . ."

"Stop?"

"Keep going. Ugh." She felt her body jerking.

"Right, legs apart still." He worked his way up her body, kissing until he got to her mouth. "It's okay, it's fine. You taste fine . . . you're lovely." He kissed her, and this time the probing continued and slowly filled her.

Pain bloomed, but it was quite bearable, and when he reminded her to relax, she let her legs down. That felt wrong, so she lifted them instead and crossed her heels over his hips. This made more room, and he slid in and out easily until she whimpered and groaned, letting waves of sensation roll over her.

"I know you want to rest, but it's not quite over yet." There was a smile in Otto's voice. "About twenty more strokes. Is that all right? Not hurting too much?"

"It's fine," she said jerkily. She couldn't say *no,* because that was a safe word.

I'll pick something else next time.

She put her arms around him, feeling perspiration on his sides. The summery scent of his skin intensified, and he paused, trembled, sighed and said, "There." He withdrew carefully, and suddenly he had a warm washcloth which he handed to her.

"Push this between your legs. I don't think you're bleeding, but if you are, it won't be much. I'll just clean up a bit, and then we'll lie here a while."

Lucy complied, and after a few seconds, he lay down again and rolled to face her.

They stared at one another, and then Otto put his thumb slowly on her nose. "Good! You're all in focus. Do you need the rest of that cider?"

"In a bit, maybe. Not for forgetting, though. It just tastes nice."

"Sore?"

"Only a little. That was . . . thank you." She breathed in, leaned over and kissed his shoulder.

He gave her a friendly squeeze.

"What would you like now? We can stay here a while and finish the cider, or I can get some dinner sent up, or you can get dressed and leave as soon as you like."

"Or?"

He stretched.

"Or, you could stay the night."

"I wish I could, but I need to get home."

"Well, then! I know you have a few days before you have to leave. I'll be at the pub for the next couple of weeks. If you decide you'd like to see me again, either for another round or to talk, or to debrief, just go into the bar and do what you did this time."

"Thank you." She rolled in and kissed his face, nose, cheeks, chin and lips, laughing with relief and excitement.

"No more cider for you, Lucy," he said and kissed her back.

"I'm not tipsy. I'm just happy. You've been so kind . . . I'll love you forever."

He looked startled, and she laughed even harder. "Don't be scared. All I mean is you'll be in my heart as my first ever lover. This will be a good memory because we'll never fall out, or fight, or break up because we were never *together* in the first place."

She sat up and swung her legs out of bed, wobbling a little. "I'll leave the washcloth in the loo."

She took her bag into the small room and splashed her face, watching herself in the mirror. She looked the same but happier.

Endorphins, she told herself wisely.

She rinsed the cloth, dabbed at herself again and tidied up, and then went out to dress. She wondered if Otto would be gone, but he was still in bed, with his hands tucked behind his head.

Lucy dressed and put on her shoes. Then she bent over and kissed him again. "Goodbye, Otto." She went to the door, nonplussed to see there was no handle. He clicked his fingers, and it opened.

"Will I see you again?" he asked.

"Maybe. I haven't decided. But if I don't come back, it's not because I'm sorry or hurt or ashamed."

"I know. Dequan told me you were a sensible person. If you weren't, we wouldn't be here."

Lucy made sure she had her keys. Then she remembered something. "Oh, shit."

"What?"

She pulled a comical face. "I can't drive. I'm on a provisional licence, and I've been drinking."

"Go downstairs and give Dequan a call. You'll have to leave the pub environs because the wards mess with phones, but you'll be safe under the trees. You can come back to the foyer after you phone, if you want. Tell him to have Kim bring him here, and then he can drive your car home."

"Kim?"

"A friend. He'll know."

Chagrined at her situation, Lucy went downstairs and arranged for herself and her car to be transported home.

Why did Dequan tell me to order cider? Did he forget I'm on my P-Plates?

She never saw the person named Kim, and Dequan asked no questions at all until he dropped her outside her parents' house.

"I won't come in . . . and don't worry. I'll go around to Gran's and Kim will pick me up. Are you okay?"

"Fine." Lucy kissed his cheek. "You chose very well. I love you like a brother."

She was still grinning when she let herself into the house.

"Lucy?" Cherie called. "There's dinner in the oven if you want some."

"Thanks, Mum." She heard the burble of the TV and added, "I'll take it to my room."

The next morning, she took stock. She felt a little bruised, but the experience had been a positive one. She decided to see Otto at least once more before she left.

Once more became four more times, and Lucy spent some of her savings on cabs to avoid bothering Dequan.

Otto came to her cheerfully each time, and they went to bed, had dinner, and once, they went dancing.

"Big, blonde and beautiful," Lucy sang as they danced.

"Who are you talking about?" Otto shouted.

"Not me, certainly, but this was nearly my song . . . I could have been Queen of the May."

"Funny old play," he said.

"Mm. We put it on at school."

"*School?*" He sounded wary.

"Relax, Otto. I told you, I'm coming up nineteen."

"You did not."

"No? Oh no, it was the barmaid." She took his hand. "Can we go back to Bedfordshire now?"

"Your request is noted."

They made love, and Lucy cuddled up to Otto. "I had my medical yesterday. I wasn't going to see you again, but I wanted to get rid of the taste of metal and gloves."

"And did it work?"

"Yes. But I'm sailing in a couple of days, and Mum and Dad are getting twitchy. They want me to stay home for *family time* until I go."

"So this is goodbye." Otto got up on his elbow.

"Yes."

"Maybe when you come back . . ."

"You might be married or engaged or busy."

"If I'm not?"

"I can hardly send you a text."

"If you want to see me again, tell Dequan. If I'm free, I'm at your service."

Lucy looked into his eyes.

He means that.

"No promises," she said.

"No names, no pack drill." He kissed her, fondly. "I still have your photo."

"What?"

"Dequan sent it to me, remember?"

"Delete it."

"No. Don't worry. Our bargain holds. If we meet by chance, it's up to you to make a move. Even if I'm with someone, you're welcome to say *hi*. I won't tell anyone about our time together, but I certainly won't ever regret it."

"I'll remember." Lucy got out of bed, cleaned up and dressed. Before she left the room, she looked over to where Otto lay in bed. "Goodbye, darling Otto." She blew him a kiss. *"Dear, dark and delightful* . . . and yes, that is someone. It's *you*."

"Walk safely, Lucy."

Her eyes blurred with tears as she went down the steps, and she almost tripped.

Catch – and release.

I love him, so – I won't come back to the Pear Tree Bar.

CHAPTER NINE: CAREY

Lucy Tan, 2020, Ferris Island

Eight years in, the camp on Ferris Island had a permanent air.

It had started out as a tent village, but by the end of the first year, there were plain slab huts for use in inclement weather. The campers and the companions built them together, using local timber felled and sawn in the traditional way.

Each year they added more, including cottages, vegetable gardens and a selection of livestock. In the communal hall they'd built in the fifth year, musical instruments, spinning wheels, looms, costumes and paints were kept. Someone at Vouch-Safe had decided self-expression was good for the soul. Making paper was a perpetual pastime because none could be brought from the mainland.

The latest batch of campers spent a full four months on the island. Some were patently itching to get home to their mobile phones and microwave ovens, but others said they wished they could stay forever.

"No can do," Lucy said patiently when a camper named Carey announced her intention of buying a new voucher the second she got back to her computer.

"Why not, Lulu?"

"The camps are booked solid for the next year and a half."

Carey pouted. "I'll just have to miss the ship, then."

"You know the rules. You sign in, and you sign out. *Robinson Crusoe* never leaves anyone behind."

"But how will I—I mean . . ." The girl's voice wobbled. "How am I going to manage when I'm back with *all that*?"

Lucy looked through the stroppy exterior and saw the frightened young woman underneath. "You'll manage brilliantly, Carey. Don't you remember crying when you got here because you couldn't light the stove? And not wanting to share a cottage with Vena because *she's so damned decrepit?*" Lucy made air quotes around the description.

"Y-es."

"And now you're capable of growing food, cooking from scratch, washing by hand, milking cows, riding, making, mending, playing the flute, and you've written down all those poems for Vena . . . not to speak of organising our end-of-camp concert."

"But I haven't got any record of any of it. No proof. No photos, even. Nothing to put in a resume."

"You knew the rules when you came. *Bring nothing but hope and a willingness to learn. Take nothing but experience and serenity.* But there's nothing to prevent you from using the skills you've picked up. They *are* your proof. And when you get back to the world that has mirrors, you'll see how much you've changed."

"I look good?"

"You could do with a haircut. You're *hem well piebald.*"

Carey giggled, touching the demarcation line between the bleached ends of her hair and the natural brown. Then she lifted her head to catch Lucy's eye. "So you think I can still be like this when I go home? Capable, I mean? Um—proactive?"

"If that's what you want, yes."

"I do. And Vena wants to make a garden at her unit . . . Oops." Carey put her hand over her mouth. "I just broke Rule Ten."

"I expect you broke Rule Ten days ago. What you just did now is told *me* you broke it."

"Am I in trouble?"

"Do you want to be?"

"No . . . but I shouldn't have done it."

"In that case, you can write me ten lines . . . *I will not break Rule Ten.*"

"Easy peasy. I can knock that over in two minutes."

"You think? I forgot to mention you have to carve the pen, mix the ink and make the paper . . . You *know* the rules."

Carey stared at her in outrage for a few seconds and then giggled. "Okay, so I know we're not meant to tell our full names or addresses and stuff, but Vena needs someone to help with work. And Sass says she *so* doesn't want to go into a—"

"That's enough, Carey. I can't prevent you from colluding with other campers when you get home, but there's no need to drag me into your iniquity. Camp Ferris is about getting comfortable with yourself, not about relating to other people." She smiled, to soften her words, and added, "Obviously, you wouldn't have time to come back to the island even if you could."

"I wouldn't, would I? What's your email address, Lulu? Just so we can let you know how we get on."

"Nice try. I don't exist to you after today. And by the way, Lulu's not my real name."

The outrage came back. "You told me it was that first day when we got off the ship. You fibbed."

"I never said it was my name. What I said was, *You may call me Lulu.* For all I know, Carey's not *your* real name. And no, don't tell me."

Carey gave a rueful grin and headed back to join the farewell party in the communal hall. She threw in a few dance steps as she went.

Lucy wondered what would happen when the holiday romance effect faded. Despite the rules against post-camp contact, she knew many, if not most, campers sneakily swapped contact details. She doubted if many of them stayed in touch beyond the first flurry of emails and promises of get-togethers. Experience had taught her how these things worked. She got to know the campers well, but she made sure she never got attached to any of them. Not only was it against the rules, but she knew she'd never see them again unless it was by accident.

And they wouldn't know me if we did meet. They've only ever seen the Camp Ferris companion Call-me-Lulu or Call-me-Mary or Call-me-Ellen. To them, Lucy Tan doesn't exist.

Robinson Crusoe arrived the next morning in a flurry of blue sails and cheerful crew, none of whom spoke more than a few words of English to the campers.

Naturally, they could, but they chose not to. It seemed kinder than putting up a sign saying, *Please don't ask us questions, and don't ask to borrow a phone or a camera, or a map. Don't ask for the coordinates of Ferris Island. Refusal may lead to offence.*

Carey, Vena, Sass and another twenty-seven campers, dressed in generic tee-shirts and skirts or trousers, provided by Vouch-Safe for this transition, boarded at the jetty. Some of them held precious paintings, poems or the nascent beginnings of novels written on hand-made paper, but they took nothing else. They sang *Auld Lang Syne* as the ship departed, but they'd have to wait until they reached their separate homes to access their own belongings. They'd be driven in separate cars, by sphinx-like drivers, and the windows were frosted.

Very cloak and dagger.

Very Vouch-Safe.

If the V-S folk ever turn to crime, they'll have the world on its knees.

Lucy sauntered back along the jetty. The island was quiet. The other companions had left with the ship, *rotating out* to spend time in the ordinary world after so many months away. Vouch-Safe wouldn't allow human companions to live full-time on the island or in any of the other, younger camps. *Time on* had to be balanced by an equal amount of *time off*. Lucy had elected to stay on until a new set of staff *rotated in* when *Robinson Crusoe* returned in three or four days' time. The livestock needed someone to care for them. She'd sail back on *Robinson Crusoe,* and a driver she didn't know would take her home to her tiny apartment where she'd take up the reins of her *other* life again. She'd go dog walking at the local shelter. She'd meet Nelis and catch up on her news. Maybe she'd see Bird Boy again. Maybe she'd catch a glimpse of her catch-and-release first lover, Otto.

He was married now . . . more or less. She'd found that out by accident. After Christmas, she'd got together with Nelis, who had reunited with their old classmate Xavier Partridge at *The Pear Tree* on Christmas Eve.

"There was an elf man named Otto, who had *two* girlfriends. They decided to marry, or betroth, or whatever elves do, and Xavier and I were their witnesses when they *called it forever* . . ."

Otto? My Otto?

"Odd name," Lucy said.

"Hm, it was short for something else." Nelis tapped her lip. "Orlando Fairling, that was it. He's something in the music industry — *Wildwood Studio* — and Kim and Charlotte, his girls, are in the business, too. They're all really close, so he couldn't have chosen one. I suppose they'll just live together since plural marriage isn't exactly legal . . . is it?"

"How would I know? I spend half my life in a kind of monastery situation. I almost expect to come back home to find aliens have landed, and none of us knew."

Even as she talked nonsense with Nelis, Lucy mentally kissed her fingers to Otto. Not to Orlando Fairling, whom she didn't know, but to her catch-and-release lover who had given her happy memories and another yardstick to measure others by.

After leaving the jetty, Lucy walked around the beach to the rugged spot where the cliff rose, pocked with caves. It was the only place on the island off-limit to the campers. The caves were properly visible only from the seaward side of the island, and only at low tide. The chances of a camper wading in and then being cut off by the tide were too high to be worth the risk.

Lucy moved to the natural rocky seat close to where the first cave would appear. She could enjoy the quiet before she started the animal round.

"Hello, Lucy."

Chapter Ten: A Picnic

Lucy Tan, 2020, Ferris Island

Lucy jumped, choking back a yelp.

For a few seconds, she thought Carey had made good on her threat to stay behind. But no. She'd seen the girl singing and swaying with the others on the deck as the ship pulled away.

She pressed her hand against her chest, settling her heartbeat. Then she turned to see August Herron splashing out of the slowly-appearing cave.

Ker-thump. Her heart stopped skittering with fright and settled to a happy upbeat.

"You scared me." She tried to hold in her smile. She was so *glad* to see him. It had been almost a year since they'd shared a camp.

"Sorry." He came to sit beside her and waved a hand to dry his shoes.

Oh, elf, much?

Lucy rather resented the natural advantage fay had when it came to drying clothing.

Mind, it was handy when Otto conjured me warm cloths when I needed them.

"I mean, what the actual fuck, Augie?"

He looked at her mildly. "It's okay, Lucy. Really."

"It's actually not. I thought I had the place to myself, and then you popped out like an elf-in-the-box. Where have you been hiding? Isn't it term-time? How will Diversity High manage without the marvellous Mister Herron? How the *fuck* did you get here?"

"That's two *fucks* in less than a minute. Unlike you, Lucy."

"I've been nice to campers for four *fucking* months. I deserve to let rip."

"Fair enough." He nodded towards the cave. "I came through there."

Lucy stared at him.

"It's a gateway from *over there*. Not the most convenient one, admittedly."

Lucy shook her head as comprehension hit her in a rush. "So I've been working here for years and assuring campers there's no way off this fricking island until *Robinson Crusoe* comes back . . . and all the time there's been a local gateway to fairyland."

He shrugged and smiled.

"Do the others know?"

"Vouch-Safe Central know, naturally. That's one of the reasons Gerry Trip chose this island. He's one of —"

"I *know* who he is. Never met him. He's the original invisible man. Um, *is* he a man?"

"Not many people have, and yes, he's a man. Pure hob, from a family that *lives human*. His daughter-by-love — stepdaughter to you — is a Vouch-Safe driver and she introduced us once."

She harrumphed, refusing to be deflected. "So all that stuff about being utterly isolated is so much elfwash?"

"Not at all. This gateway is inconvenient, and no human or tracer could access it anyway. It's quite a distance back through the cave. It debouches in another cave on the chalk cliffs, and then there's a narrow, slippery path up to a mass of furze. There's a seaman's lair quite close by. It's not a path for the thin-skinned or the faint-hearted. But still, difficult as it would be to get campers and companions through this way, it would be preferable to losing them to, say, a fire or a cyclone or tsunami."

Lucy felt her eyes bug. She'd never let herself wonder what would happen to campers and companions if the mother and father of all storms hit.

August continued, "Admittedly, the latter could pose a problem with accessing the gateway except . . ."

"Except there's a trapdoor in the floor of the communal hall," Lucy said dryly, as a mental jigsaw clicked up another piece.

"You knew, then."

"It's hard to miss. It leads to the cellar, but I spotted a secondary hatch. I thought *that* one was connected to a sewer . . . or a storm cellar, but now I think it's not. I didn't care to climb down in case I couldn't climb up again."

"That's my sensible Lucy."

She harrumphed again. "Not much use having an escape hatch if no one knows about it, elf man."

"In the event of a storm, someone would come through to fetch you."

"Huh. Did you come here for any special reason, other than scaring the shit out of me?"

"I want a private talk with you."

"Going to offer me another job? Or lecture me on the rules? Or explain your very *married* state? Or show me magical lights in the water?"

Has your wife left you?

"None of those. And I can't stay too long. Lorelei's visiting her sister."

Lorelei was his wife, and Lucy had no idea why a visit to her sister should mean August couldn't stay long on the island. She decided not to ask.

"Do you want tea before I start the rounds?" she asked instead.

August waved his hand, and a picnic basket landed on the

rock between them. "Help yourself."

"Bloody conjurer. Wait on . . . you people can't conjure through gateways. Maeve told me. And Patrice said the miracle wasn't that Maeve couldn't conjure through doorways, but that Maeve ever conjured at all. Why does she? Leprechauns don't."

"Maeve may look, sound and present as a colleen, but her mother is a pixie miss, and they can conjure anything that's not nailed down."

"But *you* just conjured through a gate?"

"I conjured it to the gate, carried it through and parked it in the cave. If you don't want it . . ."

"Oh, give me that." She opened the basket and took out a pale green cup, decorated with swags of pink and white blossom. A wave of déjà vu washed over her as she remembered holding that one, or its twin, in Augie's office the day he offered her the job. She set it on the flat rock, and it clinked. "Oops."

"It's Cornfellow ware. Tougher than it looks."

She didn't ask if he still had a certain mug painted with roses and herons. She'd had it made especially by a rosarian artist and posted it to him at the school as a surprise when he returned for the first term after she'd left. The rose's registration referred to it as *V-SRLLP*, but its common name, according to the rosarian, was *Lucy Loves*.

I was such a little idiot. But at least I never told him that detail during my sad confession. Maybe he never even got the package.

A small teapot steamed in the basket, and yes, there was the familiar *D* mug.

Augie took it out.

"Why D, when your initials are AH?" she asked since he was clearly in a revelatory mood.

"My daughters bought it from the local two-dollar shop and gave it to me one Father's Day." He patted it affectionately. "Lorelei charmed it for them. It seems to be

68

indestructible."

Of course. D-for-Daddy. I cannot *see Augie in the role of* Daddy.

"How are your girls?" She felt obliged to ask, although she knew nothing of them, apart from the fact of their existence. Until just now, she'd had no idea whether his children with sons or daughters.

He tucked in the corner of his mouth. "Bethlehem's thirteen now, and Gianetta's twelve, so they're prototype teenagers. I've been teaching and counselling teens for years, but I feel ludicrously unprepared for two of my own."

"Can they conjure yet?"

He nodded and said, proudly, "They were early starters."

"And Missus Herron's—"

"My wife and the love of my life is blooming."

"I'm glad. Truly. Glad you're happy."

"Lucy—"

"We've never even mentioned my little *faux pas* since that morning after the punch affair, but now that you're here and we're alone, I have a few things to say to you. An epilogue to a romance that never happened, if you like."

"Okay."

"Here goes, then. You never said or implied or did anything to suggest you were anything other than my teacher and then my colleague on the island. It was all *me,* and it was years ago, anyhow. Your little green elfin conscience is clean. You are utterly blameless and not even remotely responsible for my feelings."

"I was utterly clueless," he muttered.

"Oh, come on! All high school teachers must be used to being crushed on. The ones that aren't gorgons or grumps, I mean. And you fay people must be especially used to it. You're all sexy as hell, and you all smell good without even trying to. Perfect skin, perfect teeth and you never go thin on top. You never get paunches or spots, and you never get sloppy drunk. How the hell can mere human men and women compete?"

She thought of dear *catch-and-release* Otto, whose sweet-smelling body and care for her comfort had given her such happiness, but who had also set the bar implausibly high for subsequent lovers.

August poured tea into the two cups and handed one to her. "It's not a competition."

"Says the man holding all the aces. Augie, I've been to bed with humans and also with an elf man — don't ask his name because I won't tell you. I know the difference."

"I've been with Lorelei since my nineteenth birthday. She's from one of the elf families at Windhill — the Oaks."

"Arranged marriage?"

"Of course not. Unless you count us arranging it ourselves. We'd both been with other people, fay and human, but as soon as we met, we *knew*. We stopped *looking* at other people that way. I suppose that renders us blind to clues and attractions."

When you were nineteen, I was a little kid.

"That doesn't stop other people from looking at you. I bet you're still giving hopeful senior schoolgirls . . . and a few guys . . . the gentle brushoff, the way you did me."

At least I waited until I'd left school to make my pitiful declaration. And if it hadn't been for Patrice and his damned mixed drink, I might never have said a thing.

"What else can I do?" He sounded plaintive.

"How about a glamour to make you look less attractive? What about a huge photo of your wife and kids on your office desk? Grease spots on your shirt. Bags under your eyes. Sweat stains . . . Never mind. It's water under my bridge, but you might consider taking steps to avoid it in future."

Unless you like *being crushed on . . . No, don't be ridiculous, Lucy. Come to think of it, none of the other teachers advertised their romantic status either. Certainly, Jenny Shackleton never talked about her Mister Shack if there is one.*

"I'm north of forty, which makes me a dinosaur to my students," he said.

"You weren't north of forty eight years ago, and you still don't look it now. You're—oh, forget it." Lucy took a small cake and a silver knife out of the basket. "Christmas cake? It's April!"

"Lorelei got it from a hob baker at the *Pear Tree* pub. It's called courting cake, but it's perfectly appropriate for friends and colleagues to share."

"So you think we're friends as well as occasional colleagues."

"I hope so."

Lucy cut two slices of the cake and bit into her piece. After four months of plain, wholesome food which was now all produced on the island, it was unimaginably delicious. It was also charmed. She felt gentle waves of comfort and security creeping through her being. It was *safe*. Augie Herron said so, and she had never known him to lie. He was never even evasive. She was sure he'd have told her straight out if she'd ever questioned whether Ferris Island had a gateway to *over there* where the fay lived. He'd have told her he had a wife if she'd ever asked. That was the trick with fairies, so Grandmother Qin said. They'd tell you just about anything . . . but you had to ask.

Why?

Salem, dear Lucy.

Augie took his piece of cake and ate it, staring out to sea. His brown hair blew a bit in the breeze, exposing his slightly pointed ears, his high cheekbones and his winged brows. He looked barely older than when he'd been *darling Mister Herron.*

Fricking elf.

Fricking implausibly gorgeous elf.

Lucy felt her mild rancour fade. He couldn't help being an elf. She said, "Do you remember Bird Boy?"

He glanced at her, frowning.

"I mean Xavier Partridge. We called him Bird Boy at school. He was one of yours, right? Your special cases."

"Exchange student. Yes, I remember him."

"If that's what you want to call it when you bring a fay kid out of fairyland and teach him how to *pass*. And do you remember the fuss when he and Nelis Winter had a set-to at the Leavers' Dinner? And *you* mixed me up in it."

"I shouldn't have used you that way, but it seemed the best thing at the time. About the last thing Nelis needed was another elf man intervening."

"And Nelis couldn't bear to meet Bird Boy again, so I dutifully asked her to come on that first island camp. She already knew something about it. Had you had her along for one of your Saturday meetings?"

"No, but I might have mentioned the concept to her, because of her unusual background."

Nelis had been brought up by eco-hippy parents and hadn't owned a mobile phone until her late teens.

"What about him?" Augie asked.

"Nelis and I have stayed in touch. *Pre-existing relationship*, so it's okay. We weren't particular friends at school, but these days I account her just about my closest female friend. She knew me back then, and she spent time as a companion, so she doesn't bitch about it if I don't call for a few months. She doesn't drop me, and she doesn't pry."

"I see."

"No, you don't. Just before I came over to Ferris this last time, Nelis and I had coffee and cake at *The Dark Room*. She told me she'd met Xavier again. They were both invited to a Christmas Eve party by Nelis's new friend Frances and her husband, who's Xavier's cousin. Pure coincidence. Frances and Niall had no idea Nel and Xav had been at school to-gether."

August motioned for her to continue.

"As Nelis put it, *we went to the Pear Tree Bar and got on with what we started way back then.*"

"Oh, good." His wonderful smile bloomed.

"Did you have anything to do with them getting back to-gether?"

"Not a thing. I haven't kept in touch with either of them, for a start, and I don't know the couple you mentioned. I al-most never stay in touch with my former students."

"That makes me feel really special. I suppose you find me useful as a cat's paw."

He sobered. "I chose you to check on Nelis at the time be-cause we'd already signed you up for *Vouch-Safe,* and I trusted you to look out for her. I had my hands full with poor Xavier. He was in a wretched state, poor lad."

"From what Nelis said, I'm surprised you were anywhere near your innocent students that close to Christmas," Lucy said.

To her fascination, Augie blushed.

She pushed on. A bit of embarrassment wouldn't hurt him. She owed it to him. He'd caused her enough of it.

"The Christmas Hot, Nelis called it. She said that's why Bird Boy got so worked up over her at the dinner. It's an elf thing. They—you—all get madly over-sexed around Christ-mas Eve. He explained it all to her when they met up again. He had to after she walked into an elf orgy in the back of a pub."

And my Otto was there, tangled up with a folksinger and a dancer! Lucky them.

She pointed her finger at his chest. "The very pub where you say your wife got this cake, and where I, incidentally, had my first go at sex. With an elf. But it wasn't at Christmas, so he kept his head and gave me a nice time." She kept her gaze on him steadily. "You're an elf, too, so why did you risk being near all those—"

He put up his hand to stop her. "I'm a matched elf. I was distracted that night, which was unpardonable, but not because I was lusting over any of you girls. I was distracted because I was thinking about Lorelei and getting home to her."

"Not heading for an orgy? Just your own private *married* orgy?"

"I should have kept a closer eye on Xavier, but it honestly didn't occur to me that he'd be affected."

He drank the rest of his tea.

"I'm sure you did the best you could with the fallout. You always do." Lucy rolled her shoulders back, letting him off the hook. Eight years was far too long to carry a torch . . . or a grudge. "Thanks for the picnic, Augie."

"It was Lorelei's idea. She knew I was coming to see you, and she suggested you might be glad of something a bit more elaborate than soda bread and carrots."

"Sourdough these days, *if* you please. Herbed and spiced. Very sophisticated, we've got. We're evolving."

So she knows you're here with me, and you're making sure I know she knows.

She grinned. "Relax, Augie. If I was going to try to get into whatever you wear instead of Y-fronts, I'd have done it years ago. Only I wouldn't, because I don't ever mess with married men. And that's just a little unfortunate, because my darling elf man lover has married his two women, so that makes two of my favourite men off-limits to me."

Augie said, "I wouldn't expect you to mess with married men. You're good at what you do precisely because you're the way you are."

"And what way is that?"

"Oh, sensible, likeable, dependable and not too memorable."

Chapter Eleven: I'm In

Lucy Tan, 2020, Ferris Island

"Gee."

Lucy knew she sounded unimpressed, and indeed, she was.

Her tone clearly made an impression on her colleague.

Just as well I love you, you berk, or I'd have to slap you down.

He made an unusually clumsy attempt at correction. "I didn't mean it that way. I just meant, if you were two metres tall, with blonde hair down to your knees, people would know you anywhere, which is a bad attribute for a camp companion."

"Yes, and if I'd looked like that, I could have been Queen of the May instead of having to watch Liv Bellover hash up the finale."

"Oh, I'm sure—"

She snapped up a hand to silence him. "Actually, I could have been Queen of the May anyhow. Did you know Jenny Shackleton offered *me* the Bess part? Liv was cast in one of the smaller roles, and when she was promoted to play Bess, Ms Shackleton had to do some juggling right down the line to re-jig the casting."

He said, frowning, "I was under the impression you never auditioned. Or maybe that you just didn't get the part. Any part. What happened? It's not like Jenny to . . ."

"To offer something and then take it away? Well, that was my doing. I turned it down."

"Why?"

"I wanted to work on the sets with you, and I couldn't do both."

"Ah."

"Yes, *Ah.*"

"So you're saying if I'd not asked you to join the design team, you would have accepted and played the lead. Not many people would choose set design over being a star."

"Don't be disingenuous. You know I'd have done anything short of maiming and murder to spend quality time with you."

He looked pained. "I didn't know then. You'd have made a good Bess. I'm sorry if anything I did or said or . . . implied . . . made you give up that chance."

She sighed. "Don't be daft. It was my choice. You're not to blame for being *you*. Besides, look at me. I'm less than average height, average build and utterly average everywhere, and mostly Chinese. You said as much yourself just a few minutes back. If I'd played Bess, I'd always have known I was a symbol of Diversity High's need to fall over backwards to prove a point. *Look at this. We cast against type without fear or favour. We give minority a boost, and we pretend the ordinary is extraordinary.*" She paused and said dryly, "Ms Shackleton wasn't very pleased when I pointed out her motives."

"I'm sure she wasn't. But I think you mistook her intentions. I've heard you sing, remember. You're good."

"I know. But it's not reverse snobbery. I never felt inferior. I just felt unsuitable. I'm not May Queen material."

"What is May Queen material?"

"Beautiful. Desirable. Fruitful. Exceptional. Maidenly."

He sighed and sidestepped, just as she'd expected. "You know damned well I didn't offer you this job because you're forgettable. It was your manner. You always projected friendly, capable calm, and you were helpful by nature. That's why I sent you to support Nelis after that Leavers' Dinner debacle, and why you've risen to your current pay grade. You're the perfect camp companion."

Aware she was projecting all sorts of things she'd thought long-buried, Lucy said, "Okay, I'm wonderful. Thank you. I don't know why I brought up *Queen of the May*. I deliberately sabotaged my chances on that, so I have no right to throw it at you now. You may be glad to know I wouldn't do that now. I'd take the role and dare them to congratulate themselves on their *positive discrimination*. Augie. For the last fricking time. Why are you here?"

"I need another favour. Another intervention."

"A Nelis Winter style intervention? Has another one of your elf boys gone postal and got a nice quiet girl all revved up and begging for him?"

"I send my elf boys home well before the witching hour, these days. As soon as I feel the faintest twinge of the Hot, I pack them off without mercy. You know Jack Miller?"

"I don't think so."

"The groundsman at Diversity High."

"I know who you mean, but I wouldn't say I *know* him. What about him? He's not an elf, is he? Has he gone postal and upset Jenny Shack?"

"Nobody has gone postal. He asked if I could arrange for his son to come to the island as a camper."

Lucy considered the man in question. He was a tall, silent presence at the school who never did more than nod or occasionally smile in response to a polite greeting.

He was pruning a flowering hawthorn.
Wait.
No, not pruning. He was helping himself to the flowers.
Why didn't I realise that then?
Because you were going to see your beloved Mister Herron.

She came back to earth with a jolt. "So? He can buy a voucher. They're not all that expensive. Or—wait on—is he trying to use you to jump the queue?"

"In a way, yes, but it's more than that. His son is a special case."

"*All* our campers are special cases," Lucy said, reprovingly. "Everyone is special. So special that some of us have to be un-special just to prove a point."

"Trust me. This one is unusually special in a highly specific way."

"Ill? Disabled? In trouble?" She didn't suggest psychotic or suicidal, because no one like that would ever be allowed on the island.

"None of the above. But, though he's not *in* trouble, he might *be* trouble . . . through no fault of his own."

"Augie Herron." Lucy leaned over and cut another two slices of the cake. "If you don't stop beating around the bush, I'll push you off this rock. What the fuck is wrong with this kid? What's wrong with *you*? You never usually pussyfoot around. That's what makes you so good at your job, and so fucking irresistible."

Okay, so that slipped out.

She added, dryly, "As I said, I have no designs on you these days. Your wife is your lodestone, your love and your only desire and I'm sure she appreciates you. I just have a habit of loving you. Don't mind me, but don't expect me to stop. I don't want to stop. It's nice."

Augie sighed. "Better go easy on that cake, Lucy, light of my *working* life. I think Lorelei must have got Master Perry to slip in something extra strong. I'll have words with my beloved when I get back to her."

Lucy stuffed the rest of the slice into her mouth. "What are you saying? It's got poteen in it?" she mumbled.

"Not poteen. No. Master Perry is a hob, not a leppy. It's more that whatever they put in these cakes enhances and refines what you feel already." He picked up his second slice.

"Stop procrastinating. Just tell me what's up," Lucy said. She was enjoying their verbal sparring. She certainly wouldn't kick Augie Herron out of her bed—if he was single—but she realised what she felt for him had changed. She still loved him, and always would, but the desperate sparkle had been replaced with real, and rather wry, affection. He was funny, and his awkwardness on this occasion reminded her of Xavier Partridge in his Bird Boy days. Elves were . . .

Irresistible puppy dogs. I want to give you a hug and kiss you on the top of your head and call you diddums.

Lucy, behave. Remember your lovely Otto.

Okay, bad example. You kissed him a lot, too, and told him you loved him forever. And there he still is, your dear catch-and-release first lover, beloved though now out of reach.

Augie though . . .

Damn. Now I'm going to have a hole in my life where my shining knight used to be.

She waggled her little finger at him.

"What's that, my Lucy? A hex?"

"No, you berk."

Not your Lucy . . . not anymore. Still love you. Will love you forever. Just don't want you in any painful way.

She saw him realise this, just as she had. And in his realisation was sheer, unadulterated pleasure. Her unrequited feelings must have been weighing him down for years.

He could have made Vouch-Safe terminate my contract, but he didn't . . .

She grinned, leaned over and kissed his cheek, inhaling the scent of blossoms along with the richness of the cake. She straightened and crossed her legs. "Just get on with it, Master Herron. Lorelei needs rescuing from her sister. What is wrong with this kid of Mister Miller's that it's making you look green round the gills? Spill it."

Augie swallowed his cake. "Paris is not a kid. Jack said he's well into his twenties. His mum's a water maid."

"Is that some sort of fay? I don't think I know any of those. I've only ever been *over there* occasionally with my gran. Mum and Dad disapproved, and now Gran's older cousins have gone, she—oh, never mind."

"Did you meet any treefolk on your visits?"

"Ye-es. One. She said her name was Fern, and she offered to braid my hair. She'd only just met me, but Gran said it was normal and that they all act as if they've known you forever."

"Then you'll understand when I tell you waterfolk are like treefolk, only more so. A lot more so. They're impulsive, and direct, and accepting. They don't care how you look, or sound, or what order you are. They seem to see into the essential you—your soul. They live around pools and rivers, and they tend to be possession-free . . . even more so than the other orders."

"Naiads?"

"No. Just another order, like elves, or pixies, or teg. They're tall, beautiful, and they come in a range of skin colours you never see in other fay, let alone in humans. Every shade from pearl to gold to copper to black. They have an adaptive relationship with water. Their skin never wrinkles, and they can spend a lot of time submerged without ill effect. They'll share that air talent with you if you ask, although it's just temporary. They're friendly, sweet-natured and happy . . . but *not* childlike."

"And Mister Miller had a son with one of these folk."

"I won't tell you the details, because that's his business and his lover's, except to say that Fee—that's the water maid—undoubtedly wanted and loved this child. They might be free-spirited, but they *never* have children by accident."

"Unlike stupid humans."

She thought of Otto and Dequan's potential Waldorf salad and gave a muted snort of laughter.

He ignored that. "She chose Jack as the father, which is unusual. The child *threw hard to water* as the saying goes, so although he's technically a straight halfling, with one waterfolk parent and one almost entirely human parent—"

"Almost?"

"Jack claims trace fay ancestry through a leppy great-grandfather. It doesn't show."

Lucy wrinkled her nose. *She* had a distant ancestor who was a courtfolk man. That didn't show, either.

"So, Paris is almost a straight halfling, but he looks, acts and functions as a pureblood water lad."

"And this guy wants to come here to Ferris?"

"Apparently. The point is, Jack loves his son so much it's almost painful to listen to him. He loves Fee, but she is contented with frequent visits."

"Booty calls?"

"If you must! It's more than that, though. They're a loving family. They just can't live together full-time because Jack's not *water* and Fee can't *pass*. He said he always hoped Paris would be able to come and spend time with him at home, but their one experiment was a failure. Waterfolk and treefolk, and the sylvan, obviously, can't function in modern human society. The air quality is too bad for them, chlorinated water makes them feel ill, and I'm sure petrol fumes, microwaves and all the rest of it is very bad for their systems. It's been decades, and maybe centuries, since those more sensitive orders could come and go through the gates the way elves and pixies and such still can."

Lucy nodded slowly, digesting the information. "I think I see where you're going with this."

"I thought you might, my clever little companion."

"I can still push you off that rock, Master Herron. Let's see—you, or maybe Mister Miller, think young Master Miller *might* be able to function here on Ferris?"

"Yes. But he's not *Master Miller*. Waterfolk have one name. He's just called Paris."

"We don't use surnames here anyway. But you think that

because there's no electricity here, and nothing developed post-industrial revolution, he'll be all right."

"It's an educated guess. The air isn't quite the same as he's used to, but the water from the caves tests pure. The food is all grown without chemicals, and the waterfolk use soapwort themselves, so the cleaning compounds won't worry him."

"I suppose it's worth a try. Is Mister Miller planning to come, too?"

"We discussed that, but he decided it would be better if the lad comes alone. *Otherwise, I'll be fussing and watching, and he'll pick up on it.* That's the way he put it. The lad would, too. They're empathetic."

"So this is a test drive, and maybe they can have a family holiday here, or on some other island, sometime." Lucy saw how it might work. "You wouldn't have to involve *Robinson Crusoe,* because your boy can use the gateway." She looked him squarely in the eye. "And he will bolt home through it if he doesn't like the place."

"Bolting negates the purpose of the camp, but as I said, he's a special case."

"So where do I come in? I can't force him to stay if he doesn't want to. Anyway, *does* he want to do this? I can see Mister Miller wants it but has anyone asked what's-his-name . . . Paris?"

"Jack assured me his boy is willing, but I went to visit him and his mother at the falls, to see for myself. I told Jack I would, of course. I found Fee, and after we'd settled that I'm matched and didn't need her attentions, she told me where to find Paris."

"He wasn't with her?"

"Oh, no. He's *man grown*. I found him and introduced myself as a colleague of his dad's. He seemed genuinely delighted to meet me. He loves his dad. That's not too surprising since the direct parent-slash-child bond is about the only permanent attachment they acknowledge. I explained what we proposed, and I think he understood."

"You *think*?"

"Paris has been educated in the waterfolk fashion. That is, he's literate and numerate, and perfectly articulate. Nevertheless, his frame of reference is—"

"Narrow."

To her surprise, Augie's face darkened.

"Oops. I think that came out wrong."

"It did. I meant his frame of reference is *other*. He doesn't think like me, or like a human. He doesn't know terrestrial geography, and although he's musical, and can make pipes and such, he has no idea who Elvis Presley was. On the other hand, he can probably tell you the exact botanical pedigree of any plant in the pixie forest, he can entice any animal to come to him, and he knows every rock and every nuance of water. He has never been in a car, electricity to him is lightning, and clothing is something that happens to other people. He honestly doesn't see the point of covering bits of himself with cloth. He loves his body the way a top violinist might love his Strad."

"I—see."

"None of the waterfolk wear clothing on a regular basis. A few of the maids put on a sarong or a tunic occasionally, but only because the colour appeals to them . . . the way my girls might pin one of those oversized floral bows in their hair even if they don't need to confine it."

"All right. Just tell me what you want *me* to do."

"I'd like to say *treat Paris exactly the way you would any other camper,* but you won't be able to. If we go ahead, I'll clear it with Vouch-Safe Central to bring in a one-off camp with selected clients. Most of them will be straight males or committed couples."

"*What the fuck?*"

"Lorelei and I will be along as companions, plus another couple, and maybe Asha."

Lucy nodded, approving. She liked Asha, who looked like a Persian princess and who danced like a dream and who had once advised her against drinking Patrice's punch.

"And me."

"If you agree, yes."

"Why me? And what are you not telling me?"

"Paris is a typical waterfolk lad. He's good-looking, impressively built, of genial disposition and he smells like ripe peaches. He scatters pheromones about the way trees shed leaves in autumn. If he says, *shall we?* almost any straight woman alive would feel like saying, *now!* It's a gut reaction that bypasses the cerebral and goes straight to the–"

Lucy screwed up her face. "TMI."

"I had to warn you."

"Forearmed, eh?"

"Yes. He's used to living at the falls, and he takes his calling seriously."

"What's his calling? Geology?"

Augie looked uncomfortable. "There isn't an equivalent *over here*. I might say *escort,* or –"

"Hooker?"

"Great Bogle no! *No!* Sex therapist would be closer, but even that's nowhere near . . . He specialises in caring for the needs of maids and lassies and just about anyone else who wants, or needs, a good lay. He tutors the younger adults who want to know their preferences before they start courting. He comforts those who have lost their loves and puts some fun into the lives of those who are between loves, or who prefer to be single but still enjoy the attentions of a good man. That's his vocation and his purpose. He told me he can offer exactly what any maid needs. He's proud of that but only in the way anyone might be delighted with a skill they've learned."

"You're saying he'd be laying campers and companions all over the island if he got the chance, and that they'd let him."

There was a silence, and then August said stiffly, "I'm sorry if I gave you that impression. The reason I suggested couples and men and Asha is because they won't make him uncomfortable. He won't feel as if he ought to be *laying people all over the island,* as you put it. Some lads will attend to either sex, but Paris informed me he's *limited.* I think he was apologising for not offering me some loving attention. He suggested his mother would be happy to substitute."

"And you said—"

"I'm matched. And Fee said that was no problem to her, and some ladies recommended her to their men for training."

"And you went into reverse so fast your elven feet never hit the ground . . . okay, sorry. I'm sure you were fine with it."

He shrugged. "Fee was just playing with me, I'm sure. She has a boisterous sense of humour. I'd already told her I was well-catered-for by my wife."

"So Paris likes girls and feels as if he owes them some attention. And I'm the token straight, single female, at this potential camp."

"It's not token anything. You're the best person for the job *apart* from being straight, female and single. You're skilled at keeping people at a friendly distance, and you can also be depended on not to act on your feelings if it's inappropriate."

"I suppose so. I won't *come* over his *hither.*"

Augie suppressed a snort of either disgust or amusement. "I'm not asking you to give Paris any special concessions. I'd just like you to be on hand to model human behaviour for him. Coach him a little. His dad's human, but if Paris is ever going to have any kind of interactions this side of the gates, he needs to understand the cultural side of things and, possibly, learn to filter his conversation and his reactions, so he doesn't scare the horses. And there's something else." He cleared his throat.

Of course, there is.

"What?"

"Do you know Linda Pendennis?"

"No."

"She's a Vouch-Safe driver—one of the best—but she works in Victoria, mostly. She's Gerry Trip's stepdaughter— remember? I mentioned her before."

"Right. Is *she* coming?"

"No. Have you heard of Tane Pendennis?"

"The name rings a distant bell, but I can't think why. What are we playing here? Seven Degrees of Separation?"

Augie ignored that.

"Tane's a jeweller. The Pisky Waters line."

"What about him? Is *he* coming?"

"No one is coming."

Lucy gave him a wholly malicious grin.

August flushed and went on, "Linda is married to Tane's half-brother . . . pisky dad and human mother. Tane's mother is a water maid, and he's an extremely rare case of a waterfolk halfling who can function *over here.* When he was a young-ster . . . much younger than Paris is . . . he decided to visit his brother and Linda. Nobody much thought that was a good idea, but it happened. Linda got the unenviable job of *puppy-walking* Tane. She said it was hair-raising because Tane would snuggle up to anyone, male or female, if he thought they needed it. And he thought Linda was wonderful and—ex-pressed that. A lot. She and her man, between them, got him sorted out, but then the whole *don't touch, don't hug* thing got to the poor lad and he went into a decline. We call it being *soul cold.*"

"This just gets better and better. He's a menace, but he's also vulnerable," Lucy said.

"Fortunately, he met up with another halfling who was equally starving for physical affection and all was well. They have several children now. But if Paris reacts the way Tane did while trying to *suppress* his water nature, we could end up with a mess."

"And no sex-starved halfling on hand to defuse the situation." Lucy tched and shook her head at him. "I can read you like a book, Augie. Once, I would have done *anything* for you. Those days are gone. Let's get something crystal clear. I am absolutely not volunteering to step into the role of sex-starved *anything* to please you or to pander to this—menace. I will not be your sacrifice."

August's chin came up, but he said, mildly, "I know you won't. I wouldn't expect it. Just be aware of the condition and take steps before it gets too bad."

"Steps."

"Yes. *Reasonable* steps."

"Okay. I'll keep an eye on your boy and post him back through the gateway if he gets the melancholies."

"If he starts looking withdrawn, ask him if a hug will help, or if he needs to go home. If you specify *hug*, that's what he'll expect and what you'll get. It should be enough, but I had to ask you specifically because it means relaxing the no fraternisation rule."

She nodded. "Okay. I'm in. I'll look after your halfling."

"Just like that, Lucy?"

"Just like that, Augie. So you can toddle back through the cave before it goes underwater and get the ball rolling for *Operation Paris*. Say hello to Missus Herron and thank her for the picnic. And one last thing."

He raised his brows.

Lucy said, "Leave me the rest of that cake."

Chapter Twelve: Operation Paris

Lucy Tan, 2020, Ferris Island

A few days later, Lucy was back on her favourite rock, considering the wisdom of breaking at least three of the Vouch-Safe rules. There was the one about never working two camps consecutively, if one was a long one, and the one about neither seeking or accepting foreknowledge about campers or other companions. There was the one about treating everyone equally. Oh, and the one concerning forming relationships with *anyone* at camp, or afterwards, *unless* there was a preexisting relationship. She supposed that one didn't apply this time since the campers had been preselected and most of them would be paired. She wondered how they felt, having expected to wait for months for a vacancy and then being told they could come *now*, this week . . . She envisaged a lot of scrambling to reschedule appointments and commitments.

Supposably other rules did still apply, but she was breaking these few under the direct say-so of a senior colleague.

So, do you trust Augie Herron?

I do. I always have.

Elves are honourable.

Otto did exactly what I wanted.

His wives or betrotheds or whatever are lucky women.

She sighed.

It would be okay.

Two more days of peace and then it all begins again with an added complication.

She stretched, arms above her head, as she perched on her favourite rocky seat. She never sat there during a camp, because the cliff and its minuscule and intermittent beach was off-limits to the campers, but she loved the view of a seersucker sea that rumpled on to a navy-blue horizon. Watching the caves appear was magical, and doubly so now she knew they led to a gateway *over there.*

Not that I can go through. It's a dead-end to me unless I'm holding hands with a fairy.

She wished she had some more of that cake Augie's wife had sent. And a cup of tea. And Augie to share it. The pain of unrequited love had finally mellowed. There was no point in pain and no need for embarrassment. He was just nice to be with. She liked watching his expressions and hearing his light tenor voice. She enjoyed watching him tie himself in knots to avoid causing unhappiness or harm. Augie was out of bounds for one-on-one companionship, but she wished she had someone similar but unattached. It was too late to think of Otto.

We might have made a go of it, but I chose to catch and release. Why did I do that? Why do I give up something I want for something that can let me down?

She loved her job with a passion, but it played hob with relationships. No boyfriend would like being left alone for weeks or months on end while she *messed about on an island full of losers.* That was a direct quote from the one disgruntled lover she'd tried to keep past what she thought of as *shore leave.* Once she'd ascertained that he really had said that, and that her ears hadn't misled her, he abruptly became an *ex-*lover. She discovered he'd brought substitute Lucies to her flat while she was away. She changed the locks, and then she changed the flat.

Not every relationship broke up dramatically, because after that affair she returned to *catch and release.* She didn't involve Dequan after the first time but went out with friends of friends, or people met at concerts, keeping it simple and never committing to anything beyond the next week.

Usually, she returned to the world — which she hesitated to call *civilisation* — to find her previous man had farewelled her by text or message . . . which she'd naturally never got . . . and moved on weeks earlier.

I need a man I can put in cold storage . . . or maybe one with an off switch. Dammit, when I get home, I'm going to find me an elf.

"I wish!"

"Is your name Lucy, my lady?"

Lucy turned, and her eyes widened at the sight of a tall young man with foxy hair and sleepy grey eyes who had just emerged, blinking, from the cave. He had clear, fair skin that was almost luminous, and *all* of it was on show.

What the —

Oh my God!

After a few seconds of what she later identified as *rapt shock*, she smiled, keeping her gaze on his face. "Yes, my name's Lucy. Are you Paris?"

He inclined his head.

"Is Augie with you? Master Herron?"

"I decided to come through by myself, in case you needed company." He looked around. "I haven't used that gate before. Only ever used one once, really."

"Augie says this is not a convenient one from the other end."

Paris stepped up out of the water and came to sit beside her. She felt the warmth of his bare side. Augie was right. He did smell of sun-ripened peaches, and his luminous skin looked as soft as velvet.

"It's not convenient because there's a seaman's lair near the cave on the other side," he said.

"Augie said that, too, but I don't know what a seaman is . . . unless it's a sailor. And I've never heard of sailors having lairs."

"Think of water-blood men like me but a lot bigger.

Shinier. Scarier. Frighten the maids, though that's mostly just tales, I think. Something the maids like to talk about so they can shiver together and whisper of monstrous cocks and be glad of their moderate men." He gave her a lazy smile, showing the perfect teeth all fay had. "This one is called *Lore Mor Arlodh*. He's territorial, and he wasn't pleased to see me on his path. He looks at my kind as soft, you see." He chuckled, and the sound made Lucy tense with a wholly unreasonable desire to rest her head against his smooth chest and listen to his heartbeat and then lick him all over.

That's the come hither, I suppose. Resist it.

"What did you do?"

The smile broadened. "I offered him a hug to see which of us was the harder, my lady. He wasn't pleased about that, either. He could not abide to be beaten in a contest, but to harden to me . . . no, that did not suit him at all. It would not have suited me, either, but he was not to know that."

Lucy wanted to edge away. The scent of peaches, the warmth of his skin and the hint of mischief in the story he'd just told made her uneasy.

He was gorgeous, bare and . . . *other.*

Augie Herron, what have you got me into this time?

"Master Paris, are you planning to stay, now that you're here, or are you going back home until Augie comes for you?" She hoped it was the latter.

"I don't think it's a good idea to go back that way until Lore Mor Arlodh stops calling curses upon me. He threatened me with his milady, and she's more frightening than him. She's got him tamed to her hand, and any milady who can tame Lore Mor Arlodh is a formidable lady indeed." He pulled a frightened face.

"Does anyone know you're here?"

"Mammy knows, my lady. If Master Herron comes for me, she can tell him I'm here already."

"Is the air all right for you?"

He sniffed. "It's not near as sour as when my father took me through the other gateway. That was . . . oh! very bad. Is there fresh water here? I want to be near it, although I can make do with salt if I must. Better not, though. Might turn me into a seaman."

She thought he'd just made a cultural joke.

"There are caves over in the centre of the island where there's a kind of mini artesian basin. Limestone, I think. I'll take you there."

"Good. The water will be pure." He looked around with evident interest. "It's not very different from the chalk cliffs, here. I think I'll be able to stay."

Lucy exhaled quietly. Paris appeared user-friendly so far. Time to get him settled in a cottage and give him something to wear. Definitely, give him something to wear, before the rest of the campers and companions arrived. Nudity on the island wasn't forbidden, but it was actively discouraged.

She got up from the rock and held out her hand. "Come on. Let's go and—"

She broke off as he took her offered hand in his much larger one. He stood, performed a kind of dancing turn and wrapped the other arm around her back, drawing her close to his warm body. He looked down into her startled face and gave his lazy smile. Then he bent and kissed her gently.

"Nice, eh?" he murmured, adjusting her against him.

Oh. My. God. Do not melt.

I shouldn't have put my hand out.

"Master Paris." She got her hands free and pushed against his chest.

"Just Paris," he said cheerfully. He dropped a row of light kisses on her brow. "You are lovely, my lady. I can harden like a seaman for you."

"Paris." Revising her estimation of his user-friendliness, she gave him another push.

He stepped back.

"Is anything wrong, my lady?"

Lucy smoothed her apron and resisted the urge to press her thighs together. "You're here to see if you can acclimatise to human behaviour, right?"

"Learn to *pass*," he said, nodding.

"So you can spend time with your father, mainly?"

"Right. My father loves me, and he wants to show me his world."

"Do you *want* to be here? And to learn all this?"

He hesitated, maybe processing what she'd asked. "Yes. For my father. He spends as much time with us as he can, but he would like it if I could be with him in his world sometimes."

"Then you won't get upset if I correct you as you get used to human ways."

He ran his forefinger down her cheek to her neck. "You have such soft skin. It should be kissed right here." He'd found a pulse point. "Would you like me to do that for you?"

Lucy breathed in sharply. Her neck wanted to be kissed.

Come hither . . . Go thither. Maybe that should be her new mantra.

She took his wrist and returned his hand to him as kindly as she could. "The first thing to explain is that you don't do or say things like that while you're *over here*."

"You liked it, though. Your mouth fits mine, and I felt your soul starting to sing."

"Yes, but it's not what we—humans—do when we've just met."

"You have a man who loves you and who would rather keep your sweet body for his own pleasure and yours? He should be here with you. You feel as if you're not getting what you need and deserve."

"My sweet body is *mine*. I get to say who touches it and when and how and how often. But that's not the point. You don't do that until or unless you're in a relationship with someone. That is, some people do try it, but it's better not to. It causes offence, and it makes people . . . women . . . feel threatened. Do you understand?"

He nodded uncertainly. "I'm not to kiss or hold folk *over here*. Master Herron said so, but I—"

"You forgot. Master Herron is right," she said in relief. "It's not just you . . . none of us do it on this island, unless—well, if an existing couple comes to camp no one forbids *them* to kiss one another."

"Forbid?" he said, in a questioning tone.

Lucy sidestepped the nuances of that word. "No kissing. Have you got that?"

He smiled. "Coming together without kissing is like bread without butter, but other parts can be engaged."

"No parts are to be engaged under any circumstances. There is to be no *coming together*. Do you understand?"

"I understand."

"Good. Come with me, and I'll get you some clothes."

"That's not necessary, my lady."

"Yes, it is. I'm sure you know perfectly well most people wear clothing in public."

"My people have no need to wear clothes."

Lucy's patience was slipping. So she said, more sharply than she intended, "You're not with your people here. You're with me, and this is my world. Therefore, you will have to wear clothes."

She saw he was about to argue and snapped, *"Paris!* If you want to learn to *pass,* you need to wear clothes. You can't go around with your—your bits on show."

He looked hurt, but when she started walking towards the cottages, he followed.

Chapter Thirteen: The Mirror

Lucy Tan, 2020, Ferris Island

The cottages were laid out around the communal hall. They varied in size and slept anything from one person to eight.

"You can choose where you'll sleep," Lucy said, indicating the cottages. She tried to keep her voice calm. "Mostly, we assign rooms, but you're first here, so you can take your pick."

He indicated the first cottage, apparently at random.

"Good. You'll probably end up with two or three roomies." She saw incomprehension in his face and grimaced mentally. "I mean, there will be other people sharing the cottage with you. They might be men or a couple. Or maybe Asha. She's gay. I mean—"

"I know what you mean, my lady. A gay maid who loves with other maids, and not with lads at all."

"That's right. You will not kiss her—"

"I won't. Unless she's lonely and needs a hug. I can do that for anyone."

Didn't I just finish telling you hands off?

Lucy decided to let that one go. Asha might look like an exotic houri, but she was an expert at deflecting unwanted attention. And who knew? Maybe she might like a hug from someone who smelled like peaches, just as Lucy sometimes liked a hug from Nelis or Maeve.

Better her than me. In fact . . . I'll hand him over as soon as she gets here.

Augie put you *in charge of acclimatising Paris.*

Augie can go and elf himself if he thinks I'm going to spend much more time with Mister Sex on Legs. Asha will be fine with him. His hither won't affect her, and she'll think he's funny.

"Come in, and I'll show you where everything is." She gave him her professional smile. "At least you'll be used to the lack of amenities. You won't be pining for takeaways and the mall. Some of our campers *think* they want to detox in lovely simple surroundings, but when it comes down to it, they fret for their comforts and cultural crutches. It's just a phase, though. They come through and sometimes they want to stay on after the camp ends."

He nodded politely, and she sighed.

I've got to stop patronising him. He's not simple, and he's not a child. Dammit, Augie, why aren't you here to back me up until Asha comes?

Two days. And then I'll get on Robinson Crusoe *and leave. They can't make me stay. In fact, staying on is against my contract.*

She opened the first door, which swung soundlessly on its hinges. The salt air should have been affecting the metal, but she suspected Augie and the other fay companions used a little of their fairy influence to keep rust at bay.

"This is the first bedroom. The beds probably won't be what you're used to. They're stuffed with dry seaweed."

"I've never slept in a bed," he said.

She resisted the urge to ask where he did sleep. Campers' lives beyond the camp were no concern of hers.

"You'll sleep in a bed here. Alone. Through here's the main room. It's not big, because we have a communal hall. There's a washroom and loo in through that door. Composting toilet . . ."

She glanced at him and was startled again by the sight of his relaxed beauty. Bare men shouldn't look so — so *right*.

"There's a little kitchen here, with a fuel stove. You'll chop your own wood, if necessary, but we also burn blocks of the seaweed, since fuel is one of our economies. We make food from scratch, but a lot of our meals are communal, and we eat a lot of raw food to avoid using fuel. This closet here is where you keep your clothes." She ran out of rooms to display and said abruptly, "Come along to the hall, and I'll get you kitted out."

She got him out of the cottage and walked through the gardens to the central hall where she opened the vast storage closet.

"Everyone here, campers and companions, gets issued with clothing, made from natural fibres right here on the island. We have generic chain store clothes for campers to wear on the ship, but those are issued at the Vouch-Safe marina . . ."

Oh dear, he's not following this at all. It must be just so much noise to him.

"You can choose something from this closet to put on. We don't have your measurements, but I expect the things on the top shelves will fit," she said.

She stopped talking at last and watched him, but he wasn't even looking at the clothing. Most campers were curious and even a bit excited about wearing a whole new Camp Ferris wardrobe. Paris seemed to be actively avoiding the concept, cringing away from the whole idea.

"These clothes are based on nineteenth-century patterns, but we've made them a lot more comfortable. What I'm wearing looks like a gown, but it's a walking skirt with a separate top. The apron is practical, with reinforced pockets."

She smoothed her hands down her hips, feeling suddenly self-conscious.

"Not that I'm suggesting you should wear skirts and blouses, unless you want to, of course. Most of our men choose drawstring trousers or shorts with shirts, although a few like the kilts or tunics or sulus. The underwear has drawstrings, too . . ."

He was still looking everywhere *but* at the clothing.

"Paris."

"Yes, my lady?"

"Lucy. Just Lucy."

"Lucy, who should be made of light, but who is so heavy with all this . . ." He gestured at the clothing, the hall and, possibly, at the weight of her human existence.

"Why are you called Paris? Is it a place your father likes?" she countered.

He shook his head. "My mammy chose it. Paris was a prince of Troy. My people enjoy classical names. The lads, that is. The maids have simpler names. I don't know why, but it's our tradition."

"Well, Prince Paris, you chose to come here, and you agreed to listen to what I tell you, so please focus and pick out some clothing." She slapped the shelf for emphasis, and a pair of soft cream pants fell down.

"These look like pixie britches," Paris said, bending to retrieve them. He rubbed the cloth between his fingers. "Flax, grown by running water and made up—oh, two years ago. The thread is braeside wool."

Are you guessing, or do you really know?

Lucy hurried to take advantage of the first interest he'd shown in any of the clothing. "They'd probably fit you. The style is very forgiving. We try to have relaxed fits, so no one feels sidelined if they happen to be—um—a non-standard size or shape."

Paris, still rubbing the cloth, turned slowly to stare at her.

I'm not surprised. I'm babbling like an idiot.

She got up on her toes to reach for a shirt in a dull shade of sage green. Most redheads looked good in green.

Damn. I ought to put him in bright lolly-pink. Making him look good isn't a good idea.

Paris leaned up from behind her to stay her hand. "Not that one, Lucy." His fingers brushed a blue one. "Woad dye. I like this," he remarked and took it down.

Lucy froze. His voice was perfectly natural, but even through her voluminous clothing, she felt the outline of his lithe, warm body.

She swallowed, and he stepped back with a hiss of indrawn breath. Lucy turned slowly to face him and found him looking troubled.

"That was something else I shouldn't do, mistress?"

"*Lucy*. And not *mistress* or *my lady* in any case. I'm human," she reminded him.

"Mostly," he said, reaching out as if to touch her cheek. He dropped his hand to his side.

"And I suppose you can tell me which bit of me isn't," she said with a spurt of anger.

He looked her over. "Court, I should say. Most courtfolk ladies have fair hair, but you have the carriage and the beautiful line of neck and shoulder. Courtfolk ladies are musical and proud. I know a lovely courtfolk lady who wears a green gown. Her name is Yvanne, and I gave her some pipes to play."

Who? What? He couldn't possibly have known my pedigree.

"Okay, what's the rest of me?"

He shrugged. "Human . . . and possibly a touch of hob right back. Do you like having your arse rubbed?"

"I have no idea. And *please* don't say things like that. It's not—I mean, some humans do it, but it's considered crass. Coarse. And you don't want to be crass."

"It's crass to rub a maid's arse when it will bring us both so much pleasure?"

"What consenting adults get up to in private is fine, but you shouldn't say things like that to anyone you just met. And don't say them at all on this island."

He looked down at the shirt and pants.

"You'll need underwear," Lucy prompted. She took down a pair of soft linen drawers. "Do you know how to put them on?"

She blushed. *He's not four years old!*

Paris ran one finger down his cheek and was suddenly wearing the clothing.

Lucy couldn't repress a squeak of shock. Although they were discreet about it, she'd seen Augie Herron and a few of the other companions conjure doors open or fetch small items in an instant. Apart from Otto, she'd never seen anyone dress like that.

Paris looked down at himself. "Does this please you?"

Lucy opened the door to the other side of the wardrobe and carefully removed the blank wooden lining to reveal a full-length pier glass. "This is a mirror, so you can see yourself."

He smiled. "I know what a mirror is. My father brought one for my mammy because he wanted to paint her twice over. He brings her flowers, too. Why do you hide this?"

She shrugged. "It's policy. Camp Ferris concentrates on breaking down old habits and old routines. After the mirror was installed, we found some campers fretting because they didn't like the look of their faces without make-up or their hair without what they call *products*. Patrice covered the mirror, but I thought you might want to see yourself. How do you like your outfit?"

She indicated his reflection.

He glanced at himself and then away and then, slowly, back again, examining the clothing with apparent fascination.

"It suits you. That blue is perfect on you," Lucy said.

She thought he might be pleased with the compliment, but his pale skin suffused with a dull blush and he dropped his gaze.

"What is it? Did I say something wrong?"

He looked back at himself and then said with a rush, "Mistress Lucy, you said I am to wear clothing because I am in the human world now."

"That's right," she said, still puzzled.

"I understand but—" He turned to look at her, stepped well back, and lifted his hand swiftly to his cheek.

Lucy gasped in shock as her outer clothing vanished to re-appear in a tidy heap at his feet. She was still decently clad in a calico shift and laced bodice, but she knew he could just as well whip those off, too. She stumbled back, clutching at her bodice. "You—you—"

Paris looked her over for a couple of seconds and then touched his cheek again.

Lucy cringed, but her clothing reassembled itself.

"What the *fuck*?"

He turned away. "If you came to the falls, where I live, do you think I'd make you strip bare just because *you're in my world now*?"

"I have no idea."

"I wouldn't. None of us would. I told you that my people don't wear clothing. It would be a nuisance in water, and our skin needs no protection. Folk who visit us just to be friendly wear whatever they like. We don't mind. Most of us don't even notice if a friend is clothed or bare. Folk who come to us for play, or for easing, or just to swim, take their clothing off. But we would never *tell* them to do it. My father goes bare from choice when he comes to us. Sometimes he feels cold, so my mother keeps a braeside wool blanket, especially for him. She joins him under it, to be friendly. If he wanted to keep his clothes on, she might think it was sad because she likes to see his body, but she would *never* say he had to be bare."

Lucy sighed. "So you think I've been unkind. You're of-fended and upset."

"No, my lady. *I* have been unkind. I should not have re-moved your clothing without your request."

"No. It made me frightened, in case you took off the rest. But I suppose, to you, being made to put some on is just as bad."

He looked away again.

There's something else to this. Something else is bothering him.

"Paris, listen." She went over to him and touched his arm gently. "I do understand what you mean. But the situations are different."

"No."

"Yes. Your people are happy to let others wear as much or as little as they like. Is that right?"

He nodded.

"It doesn't make you feel uncomfortable to see me wearing these things? You don't feel threatened?" She gestured to her resumed garments.

He gave a faint smile. "No, my lady. I'm used to seeing brae lassies and elves and others wearing clothes. Hob maids wear more cloth than three other maids put together."

"But you see, it *does* make humans . . . most humans . . . uncomfortable to see someone wearing nothing in a social situation. Some people *would* find it threatening."

"Why?"

Oh, Lord . . .

She swallowed, trying not to breathe in his scent.

"Paris, you, or any other waterfolk man, would *never* force yourself on a woman, would you?"

She saw he didn't understand, so she tried again. "August Herron, your father's friend, told me what you do for people who want or need it. You make them feel happy and comforted, right?"

"I can squeal any maid in any way or any time she wants, and I am fast to recover," he said.

Squeal. Oh. My. God.

He added, "Some of them who come to me don't want to squeal. They just want to be cuddled, so that's what we do. I give them warmth. Some of them want to cry on my chest until they feel better. They're the ones who have lost someone. They miss being held, and so I hold them. They feel the warmth, and then they remember and feel sad, and then they cry. Sometimes they come back again and again, and one day they're finished with crying and I love them however they like."

"I see, I think. That's what you do. It's a service job, the same as my work here. And I'm sure you're good at it."

"Oh, I am *very* good at it," he said with a sudden grin.

"But you'd never try to *squeal* a woman who didn't want it. Or who shouldn't have it . . ."

"There are plenty who want it. They come to the falls to me. I never need to go looking for them."

"I expect your people, and the ones who come to you, know all that. So when they see you, or any other men like you, without clothes on, they don't even begin to think you might grab them and . . . and . . ."

"No. Mind you, my mammy grabs men and pushes them into the pool and then jumps in with them, but only the ones who want it. They love it. It makes them feel wanted."

"What about your father, though?"

He nodded vigorously.

"I mean, doesn't he mind when she grabs other men?"

"Why should he? It's what she does. Same as I do what I do. But with my father, it's special. They love one another, so they sleep under the blanket, after. Same as London and Kin do, only not with a blanket."

"London?" she said faintly.

Paris and London? Really?

"He's my friend. We used to spend all our time together, but then Kin chose him to make Lara with her. Now London is mostly with them. They are happy, but I miss our talks."

Lucy felt as if she'd fallen down the rabbit hole without the benefit of Alice. She shook her head in an attempt to clear it. "Paris, I don't know these people. Maybe we should stick to the subject at hand. The other campers and companions will feel more comfortable if you wear clothes. Will you do that for me?"

"I will if it will make you happy. But—"

"But what?" she asked suspiciously.

"After I spend time here learning human ways, if I please you, will you come to the falls? You can meet Mammy and see for yourself how we live."

It crossed her mind to say *no,* that she was not allowed to spend time with a camper after the camp ended unless there was a pre-existing relationship.

And then it occurred to her that she and Paris *would* have a pre-existing relationship. Camp hadn't officially begun yet.

"If I come, I won't have to do anything I don't want to do?"

"Never. If lad or maid invites you to *play,* you can say yes, or no, or *only a hug.*"

"All right then, I'll come, if you still want me," she said recklessly.

He started towards her, but she put up both hands and backed away. "You'll need another set of clothes. Pick those out now."

She thought he'd just grab another set from the shelf, but he took his time, choosing a darker pair of pants and the green shirt he'd rejected. "You wanted me to wear this one?"

"I don't mind which one you wear. I just thought most redheads liked to wear green."

"This redhead likes to wear nothing," he reminded, but he put the green shirt back and picked up one in the same cream cambric as her blouse. "Does this please you?"

"That's fine." She wanted to say it wasn't her he needed to please, but she was weary of trying to explain things she didn't entirely understand herself. Mostly, she felt cross with Paris's human father.

If he wanted a son to go to the pub with, he should have had him with a human woman.

She tried and failed to think of Paris at a typical pub. He might be okay in *The Pear Tree,* but that was in Sydney where he'd find it difficult to breathe.

Sydney's air quality is good, for a big city . . . but I suppose all those millions of particles in the air are the problem.

Paris touched his cheek, swapping clothes in an instant, and examined himself in the looking glass.

Lucy thought he seemed uneasy about his appearance, but at least he was resigned to wearing clothes on the island.

"I'm going to see to the cows now. You can come with me or do whatever else you want," she said.

"I'll come with you. When you have time, will you tell me where to find the water caves?"

"I'll take you there soon," she said. She reached up to re-fit the wooden screen across the mirror, but Paris took it from her and conjured it into place.

CHAPTER FOURTEEN: LORELEI

Lucy Tan, 2020, Ferris Island

August Herron arrived on Ferris Island late the next day. He came to the hall hand in hand with a tall willowy woman whom Lucy knew must be his wife. They were already wearing camp-style clothing. The ship was not in port, so they must have come through from *over there*.

She wondered how they'd fared with the territorial seaman.

"Hello, Lucy, and greet you, Paris," the woman said, smiling.

"Greet you, mistress." Paris took a step towards her and then stopped, glancing at Lucy as if for permission

Lorelei Herron had slightly pointed ears, high cheekbones like her husband's, and a friendly smile. She offered her hand to Lucy, but not to Paris.

Her smile broadened as she saw Lucy's disapproval. "Paris is a water lad. If I offer him my hand, he's likely to take it as an invitation, and I'd just as soon not get turned on in public. Did my husband not warn you about that?"

Lucy wondered if she should be offended on Paris's behalf but reminded herself Lorelei was merely stating a fact.

After all these years of untroubling the troubled, I should know how deeply ingrained cultural conditioning is. That's one of the reasons campers have to leave all their clothing and belongings in lockers at the marina.

It occurred to her that Paris, alone among all the other

campers she'd mentored over the years, had adhered to the *bring nothing* rule as a matter of course. Most people thought of it as a general guideline rather than a condition of boarding *Robinson Crusoe*.

No, you can't bring your mobile phone, mini spy cam, lucky pink socks, comfort reading, journal, photo of your grandma . . . nothing really does mean nothing. *As in no thing. Not a thing.*

But . . .

You signed the declaration of understanding, acknowledgment and compliance when you paid your fee. I understand and agree that I will bring nothing with me aboard the sailing ship, *Robinson Crusoe*.

Things stuffed in pockets or wearable luggage are still things. *That's why the chain store travel clothing has no pockets.*

The list of things campers-elect had tried to smuggle to Ferris Island made required reading for any new companion, and the older ones had informal contests to see who had sighted the most extensive collection.

The only exceptions to the rule were wedding or engagement rings, plain earrings and essential medication, which had to be accompanied by a proof-of-prescription.

"It's like bloody prison!" Carey had complained on her stroppy first day as she piled sixteen *but-it's-only* items into a locker at the marina.

"Of course, it's not. You chose to be here," Lucy had reminded.

And you, or someone, paid for the privilege.

"No, you don't keep a key to the locker. You register your thumbprint at the desk. That way, you have nothing to remember and nothing to lose."

Lucy wondered how much Jack Miller had paid for Paris. *Just what he can afford on a groundsman's wages, or what the traffic will bear?* And, *why on earth did Augie agree to this? Why did I?*

She had no idea what a groundsman earned. She and the other companions were well paid, considering they had no personal expenses while on camp, but she would have thought twice about buying a four-month ticket to Ferris.

I can still hand him over to Asha. She'll look after him, and she won't be so impatient because she won't be turned on.

She realised Lorelei was watching her with a quizzical expression.

"My husband did warn you about waterfolk?" Lorelei repeated.

"Oh. Yes." Paris was still looking at her, so she felt constrained to add, "It's fine, anyway, right, Paris? No problems."

"What, no *ad hoc* cuddles or sudden desires to throw him down and have your way with him?"

Lucy raised her brows, and Lorelei smiled. "I see my husband was right about you, Lucy. He said you were the queen of the *I disapprove of what you said and so I will refuse to give you the satisfaction of acknowledging you said it.* Well done. If anyone can resist the delightful Paris, it's you."

Paris said, "Lucy has explained things to me. I know if you offer your hand *here* it's no more than a gesture of *greet you.*"

"In that case, I shall gladly offer you my hand. Just dial down." Lorelei reached out a hand, and Paris clasped it lightly, smiled, and released her.

Lorelei turned her delighted eyes to her husband. "Augie, I'm impressed! Lucy is a marvel."

Paris glanced down at himself. "I hope you're also impressed that I'm clad, mistress."

"I am, dear. You could almost *pass* for human, looking like that, if you wanted to."

Paris again sought permission, or possibly approval, from Lucy, who felt suddenly unwell.

What the fuck are we trying to do? What is this poor guy's father trying to do? He's not a performing dog to be patted and given a treat if he walks on his hind legs. Why the fuck should he have to dial down?

She was sure none of this showed in her face. Nevertheless, Paris's expression changed from hopeful to fixed and intent. He took a step towards her and then paused and retreated.

In her confusion, Lucy saw August and his wife exchange glances. Some kind of wordless communication was going on. She knew they'd been married since they were very young, but now she *knew,* in a deeper sense, just how firmly coupled they were.

Fricking elves. No wonder she doesn't care if he meets me for a tête-à-tête over charmed cake and nostalgia tea.

She cleared her throat and deliberately broke the moment.

"It's lovely to meet you, at last, Lorelei. I wanted to thank you in person for the cake and tea you sent when Augie came to tell me to expect Paris. Now — are you two here to stay, or did you just come to check up on us?"

Lorelei didn't miss a beat. "We went *over there* to bring Paris to the island before the others come, but his mother told us he'd come through already on his own."

"We might as well stay on. The ship will be here in the morning," Augie said.

And I might be leaving on her.

"How many did you get?" Lucy asked.

"It was short notice, but we have a dozen or so. Not everyone could clear their calendar."

A dozen or so was insufficient for good group dynamics, but Lucy reminded herself this lot was preselected anyway. And the projected two weeks was barely enough for the time-less *Camp Ferris effect* to set in.

"It's a pre-existing group, actually — they call themselves the Mini-Mal-Lists," Lorelei said, making the syllables clear.

"Small illness list?" Lucy hazarded.

"Indeed. They believe . . . or pretend to believe . . . that espousing an uncluttered lifestyle away from what they call *toxic humanity* will result in good physical and mental health," Augie said.

Lucy shook her head at him. "No need to sound so superior, Augie. You wouldn't recognise an illness if it stripped off and danced around you like a dervish singing *I Shall Overcome* and giving the finger to your white blood cells. You can't *get* sick."

Something occurred to her then, and she frowned. She was about to put it to Augie and Lorelei when she realised she was being patronising again.

"Do you ever get sick, Paris? Ill, I mean? I know fairies don't, but your dad's human. Are you likely to get sick if someone comes to camp with a virus? Usually, there are medical checks, but this camp was arranged without much notice."

Lorelei opened her mouth to speak, but Augie touched her hand, and she closed it again.

Paris said, "Never. I know what you mean. When I was a tiddler, my father came to see us for a week. When he'd been with us for two days, he said he had a prickly throat, and that meant he must be getting a cold. He was worried. He knew my mother couldn't get sick, but he was afraid I would. He said human children with colds feel bad for a few days and then feel better, but he thought I might die . . . because I'd never been what he called *exposed* to colds."

"What happened?" Lorelei asked with what sounded like professional curiosity.

Paris shrugged. "Nothing. My father felt better after a few days. Mammy gave him sweetwood juice."

Lorelei turned to Lucy. "That's what usually happens with halflings. Some get colds, but just as sniffles that never really develop. Quarterlings do, too. Once you get down to trace fay, all bets are off. Some react like humans and some like fay. I know a trace pixie I'd almost swear was a pureblood."

"Most of the traces are healthier than pure humans, but not so much so that others notice," Augie said.

"Unfortunately, the only way to pass on our superior resistance to disease is via direct genetic descent," Lorelei said.

"I beg your pardon?"

"Back in the nineteen-forties and fifties, a couple of doctors experimented with blood donated by purebloods. They did it quietly, as you may imagine, but someone in my family was friends with the sister of one of the doctors—she married an elf man, but I believe the blood donation came from a pixie boyfriend she had at one time. After transfusion into test subjects, the pixie blood simply reverted to human standard."

"Lorelei's a doctor," August said.

"Hmph." Lucy wondered how much empathy a doctor could have if she was unable to catch communicable diseases. But then, it would be a handy attribute for someone constantly encountering sick people. "What do you do about sick leave?" she asked.

Augie looked nonplussed.

"Most people have a few sick days every year. Does the school notice you never take any?"

"No one's ever mentioned it to me," Augie said.

"No one cares anyway. If someone asks if I've had the cold or flu or whatever's going around, I just say no. If they press, I say I have an excellent immune system. It's perfectly true," Lorelei said.

Paris said gently, "Don't be troubled about me, my lady."

"I won't, then," she said.

Not on that account, anyway.

Chapter Fifteen: Just a Hug

Lucy Tan, 2020, Ferris Island

The rest of the campers and companions arrived after breakfast the next day. Lucy was disappointed to find Asha not among them.

Damn. Now I'll have to stay on Paris watch.

The companions must have been briefed, because none of them evinced surprise to find four people already in residence. There was the usual allocating of cottages and clothing, and the usual declarations about how quiet it was and how wonderful to be cut off from the hurly-burly of the outside world.

Lucy fell into her habitual greeting and overseeing mode, although technically August was senior to her. She asked for relevant experience in gardening, milking, fishing and gathering, and found the Mini-Mal-Lists already capable and knowledgeable. Barring personality clashes, and the wild card that was Paris, it *should* be an easy camp.

A couple in their thirties elected to share with Paris and Lucy found another unexpected dilemma.

Should she warn them about who and what he was?

But that suggests he's dangerous in some way.

You'd tell people if they were sharing with a diabetic or an epileptic, so they'd know what to do if the person had a hypo or a seizure.

He doesn't have that kind of condition. He doesn't have any condition. You wouldn't expect people to warn potential roomies that you have Chinese ancestry and so might feel the need to make offer-ings to hungry ghosts. Not that you do.

After arguing the point with herself for a while, she did what she'd done when the question of contagion arose.

The newcomers left the cottage to join the rest of their group. Paris made to follow them out, but Lucy called him back. "Paris, would you stay back with me for a bit?"

She almost heard the echo of Jenny Shackleton's voice. *Lucy, a word.*

Paris turned to her eagerly, hands outstretched. "What do you need me to do?"

She sat on the low settle in the main room and patted the seat beside her. "You don't need to do anything. I just want to talk to you."

He sat down, and the scent of sun-warmed fruit bathed her senses. It was relaxing, redolent of sunny days under a per-gola. She was anything but relaxed.

"Have I done something wrong, my lady?" he asked.

"No. *No*, of course not! I want to know if you're okay with sharing with Farne and Lila."

"Sharing?"

"Sharing the cottage. They're a couple."

He shrugged, and the movement drew her reluctant atten-tion to his flexible shoulders. The blue shirt fitted him per-fectly. "I won't offer to play with either of them. I'll keep my clothes on. If they play together, I'll pretend I don't notice."

"Would you notice?"

"Yes."

She blew out her cheeks. "Thank you. I was going to tell them about you, but then I thought I should talk to you in-stead."

"I promise I won't shame you or my father."

Lucy felt another rush of distress and Paris turned to her instantly.

"There's no need to be afraid I'll make anyone feel . . ." He paused, and then he brought out the word she'd used. "Threatened."

Lucy said, "I *know* you won't."

"Then why are you feeling bad about me?"

"I think making you behave like a human is unkind and just wrong."

He was quiet for so long she thought he either didn't understand or else had decided not to answer. Finally, he said, "I came here because I wanted to learn to *pass*. I want to please you. I'll do what I have to do to make it happen. Learning new skills is good."

"You're not just doing new things though. There's everything you're *not* doing."

He cocked his head in bemusement.

"All our campers learn to do things they wouldn't normally do at home. And of course, they also *stop* doing some things they do at home. I mean, they don't go shopping, or check social media, or hang out at the pub. Those with gambling habits can't play the pokies."

"I don't do those things anyway."

"But you know about them? Oh, of course, you do. Your father must talk about his life *over here*."

"Not only my father. Plenty of folk who come to us at the falls spend time *over here* in my father's world. Your world. They tell us things."

"But they can't *show* you. Phones and computers don't work where you come from, any more than they do here on Ferris."

"My father brings photographs. He used to bring me books when I was a tiddler. He read them to me, and sang songs to me, just the same as my friend London sings to Lara. He never brought a newspaper, though. He told me about it, but he said the falls were his lovely place, and he didn't want it spoiled by ugliness."

"I see." Even after years of working at Camp Ferris, cut off from the troubles of the outside world, she couldn't envisage life as he evidently knew it.

"You *will* see when you come back to the falls with me," he said.

"About that . . . Maybe it isn't a good idea."

He ignored that.

Just like Augie. He ignores what he doesn't want to hear.

"Please, don't feel bad about me. For me. It makes my soul cold."

Dismally, she recalled something else Augie had said. He'd been referring to another water halfling, but it also applied to Paris.

"Do you know Tane Pendennis?"

To her surprise, he laughed. "His mammy, Mama Tam, was my mammy's babby catcher. After she and my father made me, I came in a hurry. My father wanted to be there, so Mama Tam sent for Master Pendennis . . . he's the one who made Tane with her . . . and Master Pendennis asked his cousin Kee, who *lives human*, and she let my father know by . . . um . . . phone. Master Arthur went to him and fetched him through, and he was just in time to lift me out of the pool. Mama Tam said he left the kissing to her and that—"

Lucy put her hands over her ears. "Stop! Stop! I don't know all these people! Just answer me in one word. Do you know Tane Pendennis? Yes or no."

"Yes," he said.

"Augie told me Tane lives *over here* and also *over there*."

"Yes."

"But when he first came over to his—I think it was his brother—"

"Yes."

"He found *living human* was making him depressed . . . I mean, unhappy, and so—are you actually listening to me, Paris?"

His lips curled in an irresistible smile. "Yes."

"And do you understand?"

"Yes."

She frowned at him, and he chuckled. The sound bubbled up, and he reached out to her, checked and put his hands in his lap.

She said, suspiciously, "Are you winding me up, Paris? Joking with me?"

"Yes."

"Oh, *you*." She put out her hands and got hold of his, and then said uncertainly, "If you feel cold or unhappy because of trying to *live human*, come to me for a hug. Just a hug, okay?"

He got up, still holding her hands and pulled her gently towards him. "Yes."

"Oh, you want one now?"

Lucy reflected later that she should have known better than to offer Paris a hug. He undoubtedly wanted it, and possibly even needed it, but she hadn't reckoned on the effect it would have on her.

She really should have. She'd just finished a long stint at camp, playing friendly but unobtainable mentor to a group of people she wouldn't see again. She should have been at home, reacquainting herself with her friends, drinking coffee in her favourite café with Nelis, wearing artificial fibres, hearing the ping of a microwave oven, getting her fix of walking dogs, enjoying white wine, catching up on gossip, life and love . . . or at least some noisy, sweaty and undemanding sex with a catch-and-release lover.

Instead, she'd rotated straight into another camp and undertaken to keep a fairy halfling out of trouble.

Who was going to keep *her* out of trouble?

Paris, apparently. He slipped his arms around her and drew her against him, tucking her head in under his chin. For a few moments, she felt an extraordinary flare of energy, like popcorn, or maybe sherbet on the tongue.

Oh my. Oh, yes, please.

She inhaled his wonderful scent and snuggled closer just like, she thought afterwards, a dog burrowing into a quilt.

He sighed, and she felt his lips in her hair as he snuggled in response, mirroring her actions.

Oh yes. Lovely. We'll have some more of this, her body remarked greedily. We'll get our hands under that shirt and undo some buttons and . . . oooh.

Her cheek was against his warm skin, and the popcorn effect was dancing along her nerves and muscles, excited and exciting. She pressed in closer, her mouth opening to touch, to taste and to kiss.

The excitement built towards fireworks, and then trembled, plateaued and faded, leaving comfort and warmth, affection and a creeping chill of shame.

"Just a hug, is what you asked and offered," Paris said into her hair. "You're lovely, my lady. I'd love to do lots more with you, but if it's just a hug, then it has to end now."

No way Jose! her body snapped, but Lucy forced herself to remember she was more than a body. She had a mind and a conscience. This was her job. She stepped back, saw Paris's shirt unbuttoned to his waist and felt her cheeks flush painfully.

Did I really try to rip his shirt off?

He looked down at himself. "I beg your pardon, my lady. I never meant that. Usually, I'm more . . . I know what I'm doing. What folk need and want."

"I never meant it either," Lucy said. Then, because he looked uncertain, she steeled herself to step close again. She kissed his cheek. "It's been a long time since I had any," she said in excuse.

Paris said, "Yes."

"Again, with the yeses? I think that joke's over."

"Not a joke. It *has* been a long time since you gave that

sweet body what it needs." He buttoned his shirt. "Thank you for the hug. I feel warm again."

Lucy sighed. She felt altogether too warm in all the wrong places.

It couldn't hurt to let him finish what we started. We're pre-acquainted, no disease germ would dare to live in that system of perfection, and waterfolk never have accidental babies.

A shocking vision of herself holding a smiling baby came into her mind.

One day . . .

Paris backed off. "I'm going to the water caves. Do you want me to bring some pails back?"

"Two, if you can manage," Lucy said mechanically.

Paris walked away with his fluid stride.

He's going to get in the plunge.

He'd done that on the first day, and she'd watched, bemused, as he stepped off the limestone ledge and settled into the clear water. Not just *in* the water, but under it, clothes and all.

He looked perfectly composed, but after a few minutes, she started to worry. When he finally came up, there was none of the spluttering and gasping she associated with breath-holding contests of her childhood.

He'd surfaced, stood up, stepped out of the pool and touched his cheek. His clothing dried and so did his hair, with the water sliding out like butter off a Teflon pan.

Well, Augie had said waterfolk had an adaptive relationship with water. She supposed this was what he'd meant.

He'd been fine with total immersion that time, so she supposed he'd be fine today. She remembered she had other campers to mentor. She tried to put Paris out of her mind, but he wouldn't go.

Chapter Sixteen: Seaweed

Lucy Tan, 2020, Ferris Island

The camp continued in the manner of others that Lucy had companioned, except the campers were more skilled than the usual selection. They were more relaxed since they all knew one another and had none of the constraints that came of remembering not to ask or offer personal information. They needed little coaching, and so Lucy found herself with time on her hands.

She expected to spend much of the extra time riding herd on Paris, but she saw comparatively little of him. In the first week, he came to her for a hug each day. She steeled herself not to react, but she soon found there was no reason to be worried. After that first time, he simply stood with his arms around her, breathing steadily. He still felt wonderfully warm and right, but the popcorn and sherbet of their earlier interaction was missing.

He thanked her politely each time and then took himself off alone. She thought he was spending a lot of time in the water caves, but sometimes she saw him talking with the other companions or campers. None of them seemed to avoid him, so she supposed they accepted him for what he appeared to be.

He's dialled down.

One evening, part-way through the second week of the camp, Lucy had retreated to her cottage and was sleepily podding peas prior to doing the last run to check the hens.

There were few predators on Ferris Island, but she liked to make sure the hens were settled in their shed.

She was startled when someone tapped on her door.

"Hello?"

"It's us."

"Come in, us."

Augie and Lorelei came in, windblown and relaxed.

"We've been to Rustling Cove," Lorelei said, heaving a basket onto the wooden table.

"So I see."

Rustling Cove was a tiny secluded beach on one tip of the island, where long strands of seaweed washed ashore. Deep beds of the stuff, dried and shifting, gave the cove its name. It was also a place pre-existing couples went, unofficially, for privacy.

"I know you usually use this for fertiliser or stuffing mattresses, or fuel, but if it's cleaned and dried it would make a good supplement for your diet," Lorelei continued.

And you came here at . . . She glanced at the candle clock . . . *Nine o'clock to tell me this.*

She soon found the seaweed question was an excuse for what Lorelei referred to as *a status report.*

"On the camp?" Lucy asked, deliberately obtuse. She tipped the seaweed into a pail of fresh water Paris had brought that morning. She soused it up and down to remove sand and some of the salt.

"On your gorgeous charge," Lorelei said.

"She means Paris." Augie seemed ill at ease. He always did when someone mentioned Paris.

"Why don't you ask him?" Lucy knew she sounded prickly, but there didn't seem much she could do about it. Having Lorelei along had changed the dynamics of her relationship with Augie and *not*, she promised herself, because she had lingering feelings of desire. It was just having to second guess everything she said in case she failed to live up to whatever Augie had said about her to his wife.

"Stop prowling and put the kettle on, August," she added.

Augie slid the kettle along to the hob. "I did ask him. He referred me to you."

"Surely he should know if he's managing," Lucy said. She wondered if she should fetch the copper stick from the wash-house, but it was a bit late now. Her cuffs were already damp.

Augie frowned, but she thought he was concerned rather than angry.

"Anyway, can't you tell? You're the professional counsellor, not me."

She didn't realise her voice had gone high until Lorelei gently detached her fingers from the seaweed she'd been wringing into mush.

"I think my husband's problem is the lad seems less concerned with how he feels about this ridiculous experiment and more concerned about how you feel about it. He's troubled about you."

"I told him I thought it was a bad idea," Lucy admitted.

"Well, so do I, and so does Augie."

"Really? But August—you arranged it."

Augie looked away, busying himself with the stove.

What is it with him these days?

Lorelei said. "I think it's a terrible idea. What's it going to achieve? The lad's trying his hardest. He's made a remarkable effort to damp down his real nature. He's shut down his love bubbles to a degree I wouldn't have thought was possible, for more than a few minutes."

"Lorelei means his pheromones," Augie explained. He glanced at his wife. "What would your esteemed medical partners think if they heard you talking about love bubbles?"

"They'd think I was referring to some kind of aphrodisiac. And I'm sure Lucy knows what I mean. You said yourself he's changed a lot since you first met him at the falls."

"He had to change a lot if he was ever going to fit in with a group of mostly humans," Lucy pointed out. "You can't have a stark-naked lover-of-dozens stirring up the population."

"I know, but I don't want a Tane Pendennis situation developing," Augie said.

"Indeed not." Lorelei shuddered. "That was years ago, but although it turned out all right in the end, you couldn't say it was ideal." She turned to Lucy. "You know about Tane?"

"August told me he's a halfling. Paris knows him."

"He doesn't *live human* the way we do. He spends time *over here,* but that's in his artist persona. People expect him to be a bit flamboyant and a bit odd. I've met him a couple of times, and he comes across as a wildly extrovert man with a truck-load of charisma. Even a bit camp sometimes. When he goes home, he apparently drops all the human trappings along with his clothes and goes native."

"He's *not* human," Augie pointed out.

"He's the same as Paris, isn't he?" Lucy asked.

Lorelei shook her head. "Oh, no, dear. There's not a drop of human blood in that very enticing golden body. His mother's a water maid, and his dad's a pisky man. The only reason Tane even thought of trying to *pass* is that his brother's a pisky-human halfling and he has halfling cousins who regrettably got him all fired up about the fun to be had in the human realm."

Lucy said, "If he's pure fay, why did you mention him as a precedent?"

The Herrons stared at her as if she'd sprouted an extra head, and Lucy made a determined effort to get her anger under control.

She said more reasonably, "It sounds as if this Tane person is *not* part human but wanted to be with his brother and cousins who are. Paris is different. His father is human, so shouldn't he have the potential to function in both worlds?"

"It doesn't work that way with Paris. He threw hard to

water," Lorelei said patiently. "And haven't we just been agreeing with you that it's a bad idea?"

Lucy realised she'd argued herself around in a circle. She heard the kettle beginning to hum but decided she didn't feel like tea. She sat down again at the table and motioned the others to join her.

"The reason Augie and I think it can't work isn't only that young Paris doesn't have the potential to live the way we do," Lorelei said. She caught Lucy's eye and added, "I'm not being patronising. It's a cat-dog situation. A cat can retract its claws. A dog can't. It doesn't have the genetic potential. Paris doesn't have the genetic potential to *live human*. He can't do it, any more than you or I could spend eight or ten hours of every day in water and not suffer adverse consequences. It's not only his mind-set. It's his physiology. Even if he survives this camp without damage, it still won't achieve what he and Jack wanted, because it can't."

"They just want to spend some time together."

Lorelei said crossly, "They already do that. I talked to Fee, the lad's mother, and it sounds as if they've been spending plenty of time together ever since Paris was born. I should imagine Jack's spent more family time with his boy than any dad with a child at boarding school would. To give him credit, Jack in no way left Fee holding the baby. He's gone to enormous lengths to have a relationship with his son. Still, all this wretched experiment will achieve is to let them spend time together on remote islands where the air and water quality is suitable for Paris . . . What good is that? Why not just go on doing what they've been doing?" She sighed, sounding exasperated. "And besides, Paris is not some malleable teenager who needs his dad, so why try this *now*?"

"Since when is any teenager malleable?" Augie muttered with bleak humour.

Lorelei poked him in the ribs. "You know what I mean, my

love. He's what—twenty-something? *Man grown* is the way they put it at the falls. I have no idea what the real reason for all this fuss is, but you can bet your balls that it isn't a desire to meet up for a day's fishing on an inconvenient private island. It may be of academic interest to know a water-human halfling *can* breathe on Ferris Island without distress, but that can't be the whole point."

"No, Mistress Herron, it's not."

Lucy turned with a feeling of horrid inevitability to see Paris framed in the cottage doorway.

He stepped inside and closed the door behind him with a flick of his fingers.

Lucy's heart sank into her sensible hand-made boots.

How much did he hear?

CHAPTER SEVENTEEN: POPCORN

Lucy Tan, 2020, Ferris Island

The sick feeling she always got when she thought about Paris's situation swam over Lucy, but she swallowed it down.

Straight forward truth is the only fair thing.

"We weren't talking behind your back. Not intentionally."

He turned to look at her and his face softened. "I know, Lucy. I told Master Herron to come to you. I—oh, this is no good. I'm sorry, but I can't do this feeling the way I do. I'm cold. I need a hug."

Mechanically, Lucy stood up from her seat and held out her arms.

Paris took hold of her in his usual fashion, and they stood for a while in silence.

Lorelei said, "*Fuck*, Augie, this is ghastly. Make them stop."

"What am I doing wrong?" Paris asked.

"If you don't know, there's nothing I can tell you." Lorelei turned her attention to Lucy. "I expect *you* know what's wrong, Lucy."

"He's not being himself. Not true to himself," Lucy said flatly.

Paris said, plaintively, "I can't be myself. You said that would make humans feel threatened."

"I'm not quite all human. Be your real self. I won't feel threatened."

What are you saying?

Paris turned, still holding Lucy, and looked across at August.

Lorelei said, roughly, "Get on with it, lad. Show her what you really are."

"*Lorelei!*"

"Lucy's a big girl, Augie. If she wants to stop him, she can always just say so."

"Can I?"

Lorelei switched her gaze to Lucy. "Yes, my dear. That's why water lads make such wonderful lovers. They *listen.* They hear what you say and what you wish you could say."

"But you wouldn't shake Paris's hand. You said you didn't want—"

"I know what I said. I just didn't want to get stirred up. You're not exclusive with someone at home, are you?"

"Not even unexclusive."

"Good. My advice is that you go off together and fuck like bunnies until you feel better, and then—"

"*Lorelei!*"

Lorelei simply raised her voice over her husband's and continued, "—do it again and keep doing it until you feel wrung out. Have some tea, and then *maybe* you'll be in a fit state to sort out what the hell's going on. You'll need Jack Miller for that and possibly Fee. And as for *you*—" She gave her husband a severe look. "You're going to have to talk fast, Master Herron, unless you want to spend your next Christmas Hot with your willy as stiff as a poker and nowhere to put it."

Lucy's head spun.

What the actual fuck?

She heard Paris draw a sharp breath and his body, which had felt so calm and controlled, came alive under her hands.

Popcorn.

Her nerve endings tingled, and she started to shake. "Wh-what—"

"Not here." Lorelei got up hastily and put an imperative hand on Lucy's shoulder. "You could pop down to Rustling Cove, but I think you'd better get *over there*. If things get noisy, it won't look good to the campers, Augie."

"Lucy, are you all right with this?" That was Augie, using his counsellor's voice. "Do you understand what's happening?"

She gasped. "Yes. Apparently, we're going *over there* to fuck like bunnies until we f-feel better. And then we'll do it some more." Her knees sagged.

"Are you —"

"Yes!" She hung on to Paris. Everything was sparkling like sherbet and lemon ice.

"Will you come with me, my lady?"

"Yes."

Paris bent, and for a moment she thought he was moving away, but he just picked her up and held her in his arms.

He adjusted her weight and then strode out of the cottage without further reference to August and Lorelei.

What about the peas? What about the seaweed, the kettle, and the hens? Oh Lord, what the fuck am I doing?

CHAPTER EIGHTEEN: HOT AND COLD

August Herron, 2020, Ferris Island

August sat staring at the open door of Lucy's cottage for several seconds.

He was so nonplussed that he almost fell out of his chair when his wife conjured the door shut with a bang.

"What—"

Lorelei turned on him with a ferocity unknown in all their twenty-three years of marriage. "If you *dare* to say *what just happened,* August Herron, you will regret it," she said. She clicked her fingers, and the wooden latch dropped home. "Get up."

August got to his feet and looked warily at Lorelei. She'd been in an odd mood ever since they'd come to the island. She'd acted as a companion before, so that couldn't be the problem. The girls were safely in the care of Grandmother Oak and Grandfather Herron who, both widowed, had unexpectedly moved in together.

Lorelei grabbed him by the shirtfront, using her considerable strength to pull him in close. With one hand, she unbuttoned the front of his pants, thrust her hand through the opening and seized him by the willy.

Augie suppressed a squeak of shock as her nails dug in. The lamplight caught her eyes, and he saw how wide and dark they'd grown.

Oh. *Oh.*

He glanced at the bedroom door. That would be going too

far, so he conjured a mattress stuffed with dried seaweed into the kitchen.

"How do you want me?"

"Hard," Lorelei said, hauling him over to the mattress.

"Just let me get these clothes off."

"No!" She let go of his shirt and slapped his fingers down as he raised them to conjure. She got him lying down by the simple method of falling on him, and they hit the mattress with a rustle and a crunch. She scrambled back on her heels and delved in his pants again, dragging his balls into view.

"Ouch."

"Ouch indeed." She gave his willy a three-fingered smack. It was so hard from her actions that it bobbed wildly.

Lorelei hitched up her skirts and lowered herself onto him, taking his length in one fast, smooth gulp.

No drawers. How long have you been planning this?

She sighed, breathing deeply, and then put a hand on each of his biceps. "You're to stay still."

He nodded.

She lifted herself until just the tip of him was inside her and then thumped down.

She did it again.

The third time, he heard a loud squelch and felt liquid running down his balls. He tensed his thighs to thrust up to meet her, but she lifted clear and shuffled backwards.

Cold and bereft, his willy probed about, and Lorelei watched it with apparent fascination.

"Lorelei . . ." He gritted his teeth, fighting the build-up.

"Oh, you'd like *me* now, would you?"

She took him between finger and thumb, stared a little more, and then moved up and slowly swallowed him.

He tensed for more of the same, but she dropped her weight to her knees, settled back and writhed in a slow circle.

He gasped, heaved and shot, but she just kept up the swivel until her eyes widened and he felt his wilting willy clenched in a hot, wet, velvet vice.

He yelped as she reached behind and squeezed his balls until his eyes watered.

Then, abruptly, she flopped forward onto his chest, wrapped her legs around him and rolled them onto their sides in one convulsion.

He put his arms around her.

"What was that about?" he asked.

She wriggled against him.

"I need you to suck my tits."

"What, though the blouse?"

She conjured the buttons open and her neat breasts pressed against his chin. He manoeuvred one into his mouth and sucked as requested, fondling the other.

"Harder."

He complied, uneasily aware that his willy was twitching in a meaningful way.

She managed to get one hand down and grab it, tugging in the rhythm of his mouth.

And then she was up and on him again, wringing every last drop of energy from his limbs as he spurted again, panting with the effort.

He waited apprehensively for what else she might have in mind, but she conjured a steaming washcloth and applied it to his bits.

He yelped.

"Too hot?" She didn't sound sympathetic.

"Just a bit."

She conjured another one, which felt as if it was straight out of a deep freeze. It crackled as she forced it to wrap around his willy. His balls cringed away as far as they could get.

"Loreleiiii! *Ow!*"

She snatched a rough towel out of the air and roughed up

her victim until its owner yelled for mercy.

Abruptly, she tucked him back into his pants and buttoned him up. Then she cleaned herself and rearranged her clothing.

Augie sat up gingerly. His balls were stinging, and his willy felt stretched. He wanted to check that everything was in order, but what if that brought forth a new assault?

He got up with care and went to remove the kettle from the hob.

There was tea in the pot, so he poured in some water.

Then he looked back at his dishevelled wife.

"Do you feel like telling me why you did that?"

"I wanted to get your attention."

He winced as his exhausted balls rubbed against the linen drawers. "You got it. That trick with the frozen towel was just plain nasty. It was also against the rules. I'm sure you didn't get that from the stores. There's no freezer here."

"It was one I prepared earlier, at home." She narrowed her eyes. "August Herron, did you remember to *hold*?"

"What do you think?"

"I'll take that as a no. I didn't either, so we're both to blame if we end up with another child."

"Is that likely?"

"Quite likely, considering the time of the moon and the state of my libido and leukorrhea. It will probably make Beth and Gin look like a walk in the park. So how do you feel, Master Herron? Used? Abused?"

"I feel as if I've just had two Christmas Hots back-to-back."

"Well, now you know how *I* feel in the Christmas Hot when you turn into a gibbering—"

He went cold. "You always said you're okay with it."

"I lied."

He felt his mouth open in silent pain, and she said roughly, "Stop looking like that. I'm *not* okay with it. *Okay* is such a limp, lukewarm term. It has no place in a bedding.

"I'm *not* okay with it. I love it very much. Do you know why?"

He shook his head, mutely.

"During the Christmas Hot, you're all mine, body, soul, willy and balls, again and again. You cling to me, and you kiss me as if you can't get enough. You shake, and your eyes go black, and afterwards, you always ask if I'm all right, because sometimes I'm crying. You never quite get it that I'm crying because you're *mine*. For those few red-hot hours, you don't give a fuck about your students or your lessons or your art or your darned *niceness*. You're utterly focused on me, and what I can do for you, and you for me." She sighed. "Do you re-member that time, oh, years ago, when that ridiculous school of yours mucked up the dates and had the Year Twelve din-ner late in December? It wasn't quite Christmas Eve, but too close for comfort, and yet off you went, shepherding that sweet boy from the Partridge family. The *Partridge family!* You couldn't make that up. And when you came home, there had been some kind of debacle, and you were nearly off your head with worry. You were babbling about Lucy and Nelis and that boy and blessed if I knew what the fuck had happened.

"When I finally got you into bed you were so hard you barely got into me before you shot and then we did it again . . . and again, and in the end, you were out flat and worried about nothing at all. And then, on Boxing Day . . . *Boxing Day* . . . off you went on the ship.

"Great Bogle, August, what if the Hot had come back?"

He poured the tea into two mugs and brought them over to the mattress. He set them at a safe distance and then lay down and took his wife in his arms.

"It doesn't come back."

"What if it had? It's never the same way twice."

"Then I'd have ducked through the cave gateway and then through the Castle Bridge gate. I'd have called you from Joan

Treadwell's place, and you'd have come to me there."

"I suppose I would."

"Of course, you would. Just as I'd come to you if ever you needed me."

"I always need you."

"Yes, but sometimes you get absorbed in work, just as I do. So what was this all about?"

"I told you. I wanted to get your attention. Besides, having those two in here was making me ache—" She swallowed. "That poor girl. Your Lucy."

"I thought it was Paris you felt was being treated unfairly?"

"He is, of course, but he could have gone home any time. He's a big lad—in every sense. If he couldn't bear it, he could have gone home. Your little Lucy had no escape route. She's just finished a long tour of duty, and you drop this on her."

"She's the best companion we have. She's uninvolved. She doesn't allow the nonsense to get to her."

Lorelei kissed him. "You really believe that?"

"Yes."

"It might have been true . . . at one time. I expect her devotion to you kept her clear of other entanglements. How long was it? Eight years? Nine?"

"About ten, I think. I never encouraged her."

"I know you didn't. You wouldn't. You just kept her on a very long rein. You should have cut her loose."

"But then she'd have lost Camp Ferris. I think she needed it."

She said sharply, "*You* could have been the one to lose it. You have plenty to do with the school, without taking on camp work. You could have resigned and let her be. Did you ever think of that?"

He hadn't.

"And yet, in some ways, it was probably good for her. I expect loving a *good* man like you kept her safe from the users and abusers. She's probably weighed every man she ever dated against you, and when they inevitably fucked up, she'd disengage before they had time to hurt her. I doubt if your Lucy ever gives second chances."

"I never meant any of that."

"Augie, I can't absolve you from whatever you think you did by mistake."

"And she's not *my Lucy*."

She kissed him again, with warm affection, and sat up to reach for her tea. "Not now, no. She's released herself. When did the shift happen, exactly?"

He didn't pretend not to understand. "When I came to sound her out about monitoring Paris. I *had* to have a straight woman in the role, and it needed someone uncommitted, and likely to stay that way."

"The *role*? As in *canary in the coal mine?*"

"If you like."

He thought of Lucy, telling him about the other role. The one she'd passed up, only to be with him.

She could have been Queen of the May.

"It was the courting cake." He was suddenly sure of it.

"I *thought* so. You seemed lighter, somehow, when you came back to me. Still troubled about that gorgeous lad, but lighter in your soul."

"You got that cake on purpose," he said.

"So I did. I thought eight, or nine, or ten years of being *hopelessly devoted upon* was enough. I'd never met the girl, but I could feel whatever it was. It was binding you as badly as it bound Lucy, and now I do know her, I wish I'd done it years ago."

"Did it occur to you courting cake was a risky idea for people in our situation?"

"Never for a moment. In fact, I got Master Perry to double the secret ingredient."

"Yes, what is that?"

"I don't know, August. It's a secret those hob men carry very close to their considerable chests. I told him the effect I wanted, but he said that wasn't possible. Courting cake just enhances and clarifies what you feel already. And I suppose, in this case, that was enough."

He reached for his own tea. "I *felt* it working on her. It was extraordinary."

"And what happened to you?"

"Nothing. I felt just the same as I always have about her. She's the perfect companion, reliable, unnoticeable and calm. I like her very much, and I feel just a bit responsible for her."

He frowned, suddenly, as the endorphins from his bout of bedding faded. "And we just sent her through the gateway with a water lad who's been dialled down for ten days. What the fuck have we done?"

"I don't know. She's human, so I don't know what will happen."

"You have human patients."

"Yes, but I don't delve into their emotional workings. I just fix their bugs and mend their breakages. I leave it to you and the psych squad to deal with the murky stuff." She put down her mug and took his free hand. "He won't hurt her, you know. He'll give her the best squeal of her life. And he'll be all right, once he gets back into his home surroundings. You know how the waterfolk are. They don't *do* emotional attachment, except for their parents and children. They sure do love their children."

"Paris's friend London has formed an emotional attachment," Augie said.

"What? Really?"

"Yes, Fee told me. She seemed to think it very odd. The lad and a water maid called Kin had a child together. So far, so normal, but from what Fee described, it sounds like a wish match or at the very least a love-connection with the parents."

"But they don't do that."

"Well, who knows what they do? You and I are not the best judges since we *live human* and don't see them more than occasionally. I wouldn't be surprised if that odd pairing between London—that's the lad—and his Kin is at the bottom of Paris's trouble. His best friend is suddenly emotionally unavailable—"

"Augie, they don't *do* that. It's an accepted fact. They'll even tell you that, once they stop laughing at the odd idea. That's why they're safe for educational purposes. You can relax and let your lad ... or maid, in your case ... walk you through all the delicious things your body can feel. He or she will be delighted to please and will *love* the whole thing, twice over, for what they feel and what they know you feel. But ... they don't love you, and you won't fall in love with them, because once you step away and the blood gets back where it ought to be, you see them as they are, beautiful people all ready to make the next person feel glorious. Honestly, now, have you ever heard of one of them falling in love with someone who's come to play?"

"Jack and Fee?"

"I'll grant you Jack may be pretty devoted since he's still going to visit her, but from what you say, he seems an odd fish, even for a human. He may be unable to relate to other humans. And I expect Fee still spends a lot of her time wrapped around delighted men, whether Jack's there or not. Does she?"

"I think so. I don't know her well, and until a few weeks ago, I barely knew Jack at all. She certainly offered me some entertainment when I went to talk to Paris." He didn't bother to detail his refusal. Lorelei knew he would never bed anyone else while she lived and loved him. "Okay. I'll offer Mama Tam for your consideration."

She licked her finger and ran it down his cheek.

"Considering she was my *catcher* both times with our girls, I probably know her better than any other waterfolk. And I'll give you that one, provisionally. She's been with her leppy man for a long time, and she lives with him at the village. He looks even more vainglorious than leppy men usually are, so she must attend to his green bits as often as he likes. Is she in love with him, though?"

"Remember seeing *Fiddler on the Roof?* There's a quote about love . . . something about living with a man for twenty-four years and sharing a bed. And they conclude that amounts to love. Mama Tam must be in her sixties, anyway, so maybe she's content to be with one man."

"If he can keep up with her."

"He's a leppy. His pride will make sure he does."

The conversation seemed to have reached an inconclusive conclusion. August drew Lorelei closer. He wanted to conjure them bare and then go to sleep, but his mind would not be still.

Deep in his conscience, he was afraid. Not for Lucy and Paris, because he thought Lorelei was right, and they would both feel better once they'd released that terrible inertia Lorelei had sensed. It was the bit that came after . . . the sorting out with Jack and Fee, that troubled him.

Once they *sorted out what the hell's going on,* to quote Lorelei, his own part in the matter might come back and bite him exceedingly hard in the balls.

Hot cloth, frozen cloth, and a rough rub-down might be the least of what he'd suffer.

"We'd better go to our cottage, in case Lucy comes back here," he said.

Lorelei got up and conjured their mattress back to where it came from. She removed her drawers from her apron pocket, dangled them in front of him for a moment, and then conjured them on.

They let themselves out and walked round via the hens, which clucked sleepily, before entering their own cottage and bedding down properly.

While they were settling, August took the opportunity to check out his willy and balls manually. No bruises. No abrasions. Actually, they felt pleasantly invigorated, even rejuvenated. Young and cheeky.

Lorelei heaved up on her elbow.

"What are you doing there, Augie?"

"Plotting my next move," he said.

"Go to sleep."

He put his hand on her shoulder and pressed her down onto her back.

"Augie."

He squeezed her nipple gently. "Not tender from earlier?"

She yawned. "No, it's fine. You're always gentle."

He conjured an ice cube from their freezer at home, popped it into his mouth and lowered his head with purpose.

Lorelei squealed.

"Race you to the finish line," he mumbled around ice and nipple. He rolled on top of her, entered with a long smooth thrust and got to work.

He really, *really* hoped she had another frozen cloth.

PART THREE: OVER THERE

CHAPTER NINETEEN: MOSS AND WATER

Lucy Tan, 2020, Over there

If Lucy had ever tried to imagine the most unlikely scenario ever, it might have been this one.

What Nelis had described of her Christmas meeting with Xavier Partridge had been told with considerable relish. Though fuzzy on some of the carnal detail, it had sounded highly unlikely to Lucy, not least because she couldn't imagine her quiet friend in such a situation.

To think she went to Bedfordshire where I went with Otto . . .

She'd loved being with Otto, but her time with him had been calm and intentional.

Now, being carried swiftly through the night in the arms of a strong fairy man, she felt a mix of incredulity and exultation.

I'm just going to let this happen.

She turned her head to look at Paris, but it was too dark to see his expression.

"You'll have to put me down when we get to the cave."

His arms tightened. "No, my lady. I can carry you through."

"Augie said it's difficult. We should have gone through the trapdoor."

The sea swished as they closed in on the miniature cliff, and the moonlight caught the creaming waves.

"Paris, stop! The water's over the entrance."

He stepped down to her rocky perch, where they'd sat

together the day he came out of the cave.

"Do you trust that you'll come to no harm with me, my lady?"

"Lucy," she reminded.

"My Lucy?"

"Yes."

He set her down on the rock, bent and put both arms around her waist, drawing her close.

Popcorn. Sherbet.

He bent lower and caught her lips with his.

Oh!

And then suddenly she was in the water, still pressed close to Paris as he breathed air into her lungs. It filled her smoothly, making her shudder with the idea of what else would soon fill her. And then, still holding her, he threw himself forwards in a dolphin leap. They were under the ocean, darting into the submerged cave.

She could see nothing but odd occasional wavering streaks. She was aware always of Paris's body pressed to hers, and her hair, loose from its bun, floating around her face and his.

There was an odd, brief pause, and she felt his shoulder flex as he reached out. He tipped them upright and took a mighty stride forwards, out of the water, into a cave quivering with phosphorescence.

Oh – beautiful!

She looked about at marvellous shapes, coloured with shades of pink and green and amber.

"Would you like me to carry you, my Lucy, or will you walk?"

"I'll walk." She took his hand, finding it warm and dry.

Her clothing dragged against her legs. "Paris, can you dry my clothes the way you do yours?"

He touched his cheek, and the water left the fabric. Her hair was wet, but she could handle that. Holding hands, they walked through the cave, which gradually narrowed to a tunnel. After a bit, there was sky overhead, and the path became narrow and slick with spray. Lucy slipped, but Paris kept her from falling.

"It might be easier if I carry you."

"Yes."

He lifted her, and she never even thought he might drop her.

They moved faster now and came to a choice of ways. Paris turned left. "The other way is where Lore Mor Arlodh lairs. If we're quick and silent, he'll maybe not —"

A splash and a surge heralded what Lucy at first took to be a dolphin, but the figure soared out of the sea and landed on the path before them. It was still dark, but he gleamed with a pearly phosphorescence.

He was huge, taller than Paris, with long hair and pointed ears.

"You again."

Lucy stared, captivated and afraid.

"Greet you, seaman," Paris said. He was breathing hard.

"And greet you, too, water lad. And . . . what is this you have? Is it an offering for me? Looks tasty."

Lucy's heart banged in her chest as he reached out and touched her cheek.

"This is Lucy," Paris said.

"Very nice, but a trifle overdressed. And you, water lad . . . clothing?"

A second figure came silently down from the path, a tall woman in a cloak. She came up behind the seaman, drew back her hand and dealt him a ringing slap on the buttocks. "Stop that, Lore, or your balls can go begging tonight."

The seaman reached behind him and used one arm to haul the woman in front of him. "This is mine. Mistress Xanthe Mor Arlodh," he said, in explanation. "As you see, I allow her to wear clothing . . . if it pleases me." He slid one hand under the cloak.

The woman tossed back her hair. "And *who* wore a fine set of clothing to the midsummer ball and popped his buttons?" she taunted. She peered at Lucy. "I made him clad himself. Otherwise, he'd have gone bare, and I had a new gown, and I wanted the attention on *me*. And by the way, Lucy . . . Lucy? What he said about an offering was pure provocation. He doesn't eat maidens, and I assure you he has his hands full with tending to *my* — "

She ended her speech with a yelp as the seaman roared with annoyance and flipped her over his shoulder.

"Mistress Xanthe needs some discipline, I see. Until next time, water lad," he growled. Then he gave a predatory but rather attractive smile and said, quite gently, "*Nos dha Nos da,* Mistress Lucy." He sprang sideways into the ocean.

"Wh-what?"

"He bade you goodnight," Paris said. He continued along the path. "He liked you."

"Is that a good thing?"

"It is a very good thing. His opinion of me has risen in consequence."

"Will *she* be all right?"

"Yes. They're so hot for one another they're probably coupled under the waves already. They'll fuck like bunnies. What is a bunny?"

"A rabbit."

"Oh."

The path climbed steeply and rose soon above the lip of the cliff, where moonlight washed silver turf.

"Where are we going?" Lucy asked.

"To a place I know. London and I used to play there when we were tiddlers."

"Is it far?" Lucy remembered there was little concept of

distance *over here*. Grandmother Qin could open the gateways, but her ability to *go*, as the fay put it, had diminished over the years.

Paris said, "We'll be there very soon." He stepped forward and then set Lucy on her feet again. Holding hands, they walked inland from the cliffs, through shadowed paths to a place where the interlacing boughs of some sweet-scented trees made a kind of shelter. A rivulet trickled somewhere close by, and Lucy perceived the splash of a cascade.

"This is the place," Paris said.

Lucy bit her lip nervously. Back on Ferris Island, she'd been keyed up and ready to *fuck like bunnies*, as August's wife had put it. Now the time had come, all her reservations and her concerns rushed back over her.

Paris let go of her hand. "You've changed your mind, my lady."

"No. I mean—"

Let's not rush in. This is silly. You don't do this kind of thing. He's not your type. You don't deserve him—

She stopped her anxious self-talk with a jerk.

"Paris, I want to see . . . to experience . . . your true self. I won't be afraid. Or threatened. I'm not a virgin, although it's been a while. I just would like the answer to one question, and I promise it won't make any difference to what we do tonight."

He reached out for her and then withdrew his hands.

"I just want to know if, when we do this, when I'm with the real, true you, whether you'll be able to know the real, true me. I know it won't make a difference to you. You can give any woman a good time. But if you see into me, I know you won't judge, but will you *know* what I'm feeling?"

This rather tangled speech was the best she could do, but she stopped, waiting for the reply.

"I'll know."

"And it won't make any difference to what you feel?"

He began to speak and then stopped. "It never has before," he said.

"Fair enough. Do we have a mattress or something?"

"Whatever you want."

"No, whatever *you* want. Just do what you usually do."

"Usually, I play in water, but I have done it in the grass. Here." He indicated a smoother area. Lucy stepped forward, finding it soft and springy, like memory foam.

"Moss," Paris said.

He touched his cheek, and his clothing vanished.

Lucy perceived she had to make a move. She lifted off her apron and unbuttoned her blouse. She took off her boots, stockings and skirt and stood nervously in her shift and bodice. Then she stopped.

"You know, I mean, you do realise I'm not perfect the way you are. I am too much human to have that beautiful skin."

"Waterfolk don't bother with looks," he said.

Lucy undid the bodice and then removed the shift. She stood in her drawers, bigger than granny pants, but familiar from all her shifts as a camp companion.

She loosened the drawstring, let them fall around her ankles, and kicked them off. Then she stepped forward to Paris, and, hesitantly, she put her arms up around his shoulders and lifted her mouth to his.

The popcorn went berserk.

Paris closed his arms around her waist, and they kissed hungrily. In seconds, Lucy felt herself liquifying. Her breasts tightened, and she moaned against his mouth. Her knees buckled, and he let his fold, so they went down into the moss, still kissing.

Lucy brought her mouth away to gasp in air and found her hands on his shoulders, forcing him down. "I want to lick you."

He gathered her loosely and let her do as she wanted. She

moaned greedily as her tongue stroked his smooth skin. Her back arched as a sudden rush of sensation came over her, and her eyes widened. "I—"

He pulled her gently against him, so she felt the reassuring thud of his heart. He kissed her hair and stroked her bottom, and she arched to the caress.

"You have hob in you, my Lucy. Let it rise—that's it." He increased the tempo of his rubbing, and she squirmed, kissing his throat.

"You'd better—*Oh!*" She jerked against him, sobbing.

He turned her around and kissed the back of her neck, hands on her breasts. Lucy relaxed into the warmth.

Oh, lovely, lovely.

Something was pressing against her, and she moved, rubbing sensuously against it.

"Let me?"

She turned and pressed him down again and fondled his impressive erection. The skin was wonderfully soft and warm, and when she dropped her face against his balls, she thought she'd never felt anything so perfect. She buried her lips in them and kissed.

Paris gasped. "Please!"

Lucy reluctantly moved away and lay beside him, gazing up through the branches. She saw pale blossoms, or maybe it was just the white-hot surge of sherbet that took over her body as he carefully manoeuvred his way inside her.

"Lucy. *Lucy!*" He thrust urgently, and she heard him sob and cry out as a burst of sensation flashed over her.

That's not me . . . not . . . it's his!

She kissed his mouth, clinging with arms and legs, rocking against him.

The fizzing faded, but the warmth remained, as something cool floated down and touched her cheek.

"Paris, is it snowing?"

He said nothing, breathing raggedly. He was still inside

146

her, and she felt him still hard and trembling.

"There's more to do?"

He took a couple of gasping breaths.

"Go ahead. I feel wonderful."

She did, too. She had no desire to roll away or to shower or to regain her autonomy. She was briefly part of his world, and it had been so long since she'd been loved like this.

So long? Try never!

He began to move again, slowly, gently, and she rocked in time with him. There was no urgency, so she gave all her attention to him, kissing his throat and pressing herself to meet him.

Slowly, the delicious comfort receded as the lightning tripped along her nerves. She felt herself gathering and pulled his mouth to hers, so their cries blended.

She flopped, spent, and she felt him relax and withdraw at last.

That was . . .

He moved, turning his head away.

"Paris, what's the matter."

"I need to go to the water, but—" He hesitated.

"But what?"

"But I can't leave you yet. There's more to do."

She sat up. "Let's both go into the water. Will that be all right? Remember, I can't stay down the way you can."

"I can give you the water gift, my Lucy."

My Lucy.

She got up slowly because her legs were wobbling, and he rose in one lithe movement. She swayed, and he scooped her up, holding her against his chest.

A few steps and a splash, and he sat down with her. Water, much warmer than she expected, rose to her shoulders, so she was almost floating. He drew a long, controlled breath, turned and blew it gently into her lungs. It filled her, and she felt her skin prickle as if she'd stepped into sunlight.

Paris laid them both down on the shifting pebbles on the stream.

Lucy panicked briefly as her head went underwater, but she trusted him. She waited for what would happen.

He ran his fingers over every piece of her skin, and then followed the same path with his mouth, drawing bubbles in its wake. She giggled, and an eruption of air ballooned to the sliding surface.

And then he was in her again, and everything was sliding in water and the muted plash of the cascade.

Chapter Twenty: Waterfolk

Lucy Tan, 2020, Over there

Paris lifted Lucy out of the water.

Her legs felt heavy, and she crumpled onto the soft grass. The smell of crushed mint and bitter thyme rose around her.

She crouched forward, her head reeling as she tried to process what had happened.

After a few seconds, she collected herself.

I'm tired. That's all it is. She straightened and got carefully to her feet. She raised her arms and stretched, arching her spine. Despite her tiredness, she still felt a whisper of the fluid movements under the water.

She turned to look at Paris.

He was standing back, and, as far as she could tell, he was gazing at his bare feet.

He's beautiful.

She asked, without premeditation, "So that was the true you?"

The awkward rhyme caught at her ears.

He glanced up and then away.

Lucy stepped up and lifted a caressing hand to his cheek. "Paris?" She slipped her free arm around him. "That was— magical. Wonderful. I've never felt more . . ." She hesitated to say *loved* because she'd gathered that concept wasn't one he'd use. "Treasured," she said, instead. "And now I'm making you all wet." She took a step back, but he caught her back against him, scooped her up and returned to the mossy patch under the trees. He sat down with his back against a tree, cradling her in his lap.

"I thought you felt bad, after," he said.

"No," she said puzzled.

Didn't he say he could tell?

Then her mind cleared. "I'm tired, that's all. It's been a strange night. Do you know what I'd love to do now? Curl up with you and sleep. It's been a long time since I spent the night with someone."

"I never have," he said, sounding puzzled.

Lucy looked up at the stars, shining through the tree. "I need a pillow."

Paris lay down and brought her head onto his shoulder.

There was no fizz and no popcorn excitement, just a warm sense of comfort.

Lucy brought one hand over to hold his wrist and lifted her leg over his. "You don't mind?"

He kissed her cheek.

Lucy must have slept, because when she opened her eyes, the sky had lost its black and turned pearly. Colour had begun to show, and she looked about with delight.

There was no slow bewilderment and no sense of regret. She was exactly where she wanted to be.

She imagined talking to Nelis when she saw her next. "And then we fucked like bunnies until I was too tired for anything but sleep."

Nelis would splutter and get a coughing fit. *Lucy Tan! And to think I skimmed over the juicier bits of my first time with Xavier because I didn't want to shock you!*

Lucy felt the chill of the dawn and snuggled closer to Paris. He stirred and cuddled her, and she felt the excitement rising between them.

She put her hand on his cock and stroked it as if it was a beloved pet.

He rolled into her, and they coupled again, with the dazzle of shared excitement bringing a cry from Lucy.

Still holding him close, she looked into his face and bathed in his wide smile.

"Good, eh?" he said, as he'd said once before.

"You have no idea how good." But maybe he had. "Is the water cold?"

He looked nonplussed.

"Can we go and sit in the water? Not like last night, but just to freshen up."

He grinned and got up, bringing her with him. "My Lucy. We can go to the cascade."

They walked along the rivulet, and, in the growing light, Lucy saw the small waterfall she'd heard during the night. It flowed smoothly down over rocks and poured into a pool.

Lucy baulked, seeing other people there.

And I'm bare.

She felt a blush rising as she saw a woman sitting on a rock, dangling her feet in the water. She had on a sarong that dropped carelessly from one shoulder, leaving one breast bare. She had a baby in her arms, and she turned to look at them.

"Greet you, Paris, and my lady!"

Oh Lord . . . is she one of his . . .

Paris said in her ear, "Do you want your clothes, Lucy?"

She forced herself to relax. "No. It's okay."

She looked at the woman, who sat there sweet-faced and clear-eyed, and not young.

You remind me of someone.

Paris said, "Greet you, Mama Tam." He approached the woman and took the sleeping baby from her arms. "Greet you, Lara." He kissed the child on the brow and turned to Lucy. "I won't be long." He stepped into the pool and vanished, baby and all.

Is she his?

Lucy's feeling of contentment shook.

Lorelei Herron's voice sounded in her memory. *Show her what you really are.*

What he really was—her beautiful lover who gave her magic and delight, but who was also the beautiful lover of countless others.

This is what he is and what he does.

And how is it different from what you had Otto do for you?

The woman turned to look at Lucy, cocking her head to the side. "Mistress . . ."

"Lucy," she said.

Mama Tam's eyes softened. "Human, are you? I took you for a courtfolk lady, though they don't come to us much. Come and sit by me, sweet." She nodded to the pool. "*No harm.* But maybe you know that?"

Lucy asked, hesitantly, "Are you the Mama Tam who has a son with a pixie?"

Mama Tam laughed. "Never did that, dear. No. I have my Becca. Her father is Moss, the beechmaster. I made my Whim with a fine hob man, strong and kind. Then I have my three lads, all made with my man Liam." She shook her head, rue-fully. "I had my heart set on a handsome human man, but he had a pisky minx who would have yelled if he'd given me a babby, so Liam it was. One child, I asked for, but he's a stub-born one, and he gave me *three.* Then there's my Tane. I made *him* with a pisky man, the nicest one I knew."

"Pisky. That's it, Tane."

Mama Tam said, "Raised a few chins, that did. He was my first." She chuckled. "My lads and maids are just the way I saw them when I planned. I do wonder what I might have made with that human man, though." She winked at Lucy. "Know what? He's the only man ever said no to me . . . aside from my Liam, and he just said *no* until I said *yes.*"

She tucked a companionable arm around Lucy, and a com-fortable warmth stole over her. Mama Tam smelled sweetly of wallflowers.

"So did Paris say yes to you? It's fine if he did. I know what he is . . . what he does."

The woman gave her a squeeze. "That one never said yes or no to me. I never asked. He was a tiddler when I said yes to my Liam. Nice, though. Halfling, but you wouldn't know it. All the maids say he's sweet with them." She added, "I know his father. Nice arse. See plenty of it when he's squealing Fee."

They sat in silence for a minute, and then Tam said, "Anyway, I was Fee's babby catcher, and I never did squeal for lads or men I helped to life. Didn't seem right . . . godmothered 'em, see." She looked up at the sky. "Time I was off. My Liam knows what I am, and he knows I come here. Still, he likes me in bed when he wakes up hard and needs to greet the morning. Even now. Makes for a happy day for both of us." She kissed Lucy on the cheek and got up. "Time London was back for his babby, too, and you may tell him."

She walked away, vanishing between one step and the other.

Lucy had seen that trick before, but it was long ago. Grandmother Qin had never been able to do it effectively, or to explain it.

She sat on, starting to feel troubled. Paris had been underwater a long time, and he had that little baby.

She was wondering what, if anything, she should do when she heard a delighted giggle and a young black woman dashed into view. She had the darkest skin Lucy had ever seen. She waved cheerfully to Lucy, and called breathlessly, "London's coming, but he needs to—oof!"

A man who was even darker than the girl caught her around the waist and jumped into the pool with her. They sank in a stream of bubbles.

More waterfolk, obviously. The baby's black, so maybe she's theirs.

"Lucy."

Lucy turned sharply to see Paris, still holding the child, standing behind her.

She said quickly, "I think I just saw your friend London and his . . . well, I expect she was Kin. Mama Tam said she had to go back to Liam to *greet the morning*. Does any of that make sense?"

Paris said, "Lucy, I didn't think anyone else would be here. Mostly everyone is at the falls or the sky pool."

"That's all right."

"You can put your clothes on if you want."

"Paris, it's *all right*."

"But you wanted me to wear them."

"That was just around the campers. Oh, shit. I suppose I ought to go back to the island."

"Won't you stay with me?"

She was torn between duty and inclination. But maybe staying with Paris was her duty. She was meant to be trying to sort something out. "I think we're supposed to talk to your dad," she said, frowning. She had a feeling it was important, but right then, she felt odd.

"Can you give that baby back to her parents?"

"When they finish, I will."

"Finish what? Where are they?"

A long squeal and a low chuckle from the trees beyond made her scalp prickle.

"They won't be long," Pari said. He sat beside her where Mama Tam had been and absently passed her the child.

"You jumped in the water, and then you came from behind me."

"There's a way out behind the cascade. I'll show you . . . Oh, here they come." He raised his voice. "London, come and get Lara!"

The young couple, arms wrapped around one another,

emerged from the trees. They both beamed when they saw Paris. The man disengaged and loped up to them. He squashed in beside Paris and said contentedly, "Greet you, man! You all right?" He flung an arm around Paris and roughed up his hair.

A surge of bubbling excitement hit Lucy, but she realised it was someone else's. It was nice. She wanted to snuggle up with Paris some more and maybe tickle him.

She put her free arm round him and bumped arms with the other man.

He leaned back and regarded her with interest. "Greet you, lovely. Want to play?"

Lucy nodded emphatically but added, "I do, but I want to play with Paris."

The dark girl giggled again and slid down on Lucy's other side. "London's too tired anyway. I saw to that." She laughed merrily and tickled the baby's cheek. "Want suck, lovely?" She added, to Lucy, "Give her to me, unless you got some milk?"

"No." Lucy handed over the child rather regretfully and the girl, Kin, lifted her to one breast.

"Ahhhh," she exhaled, and Lucy felt a strange pang, an ache and then a pleasant feeling she couldn't identify.

Kin leaned over and kissed the top of her head. "Sorry, sweeting. That better?"

The feeling lessened.

"What *was* that?" Lucy asked.

She was vaguely aware of the men talking, but Kin said, "You know Tango?"

"How to dance it?"

"No, a halfling. Nice, got a human da."

"I don't, then."

"Where did you come from?"

Lucy tried to unravel an answer to that and said, "I live *over there.* Paris brought me here."

"Good. *Good.* You squeal with him? Make him happy?"

"Well, we did last night."

"Do it again. He needs it. Needs you. He's been hurting since London and I are . . ." She brought a hand around to the one supporting the baby and hooked her thumbs together. "Never did expect that," she said meditatively.

A wave of affection swept over Lucy.

"Sorry," Kin said, and it faded.

"I have no idea what's going on," Lucy said plaintively. "You do know I'm human, right?"

"Hmm. Still nice. I expect you're catching the edge of what *we* feel. Some do it more than others. When you were with Paris, all tight together, and when he let go, did you feel him?"

"What he was feeling, do you mean?"

"Yes! Some do. I feel London. You know, we sleep together? Stay together, after? *Never* expected that."

She swapped the baby to the other breast and began to hum a song Lucy didn't know.

When Lara had finished her feed, Kin said, "London," and her man stood up.

He ruffled Paris's hair again and said, "You better take this maid to the moss. She needs you." He turned his bright gaze on Lucy. "Be nice with him. He's my friend." He bent from the waist, impossibly flexible, and laid his cheek against hers. The bubbling happiness intensified.

That's the way she *makes him feel?*

Lucy watched the little family walk away until they did the same vanishing trick as Mama Tam's.

She moved up closer to Paris. "Can we get in the water now?"

He slid in and held out his arms. Lucy went into them without hesitation.

Without the distraction of other excitable waterfolk, she

was better able to identify her sensations as Paris held her in the water. "Is it always like that?" she asked, leaning into his warmth.

"It?"

"Your friends. I kept feeling odd things, and Kin said I was feeling what they were."

"They're not what Mistress Herron calls *dialled down*," he said.

"It's nice." She realised he'd closed off to her and kissed his neck. "You don't have to dial down with me. Not here. How do you do that, anyway?"

"I don't know. I just do. We can all do it, but mostly only with people who aren't water and never for long."

"I don't need you to do that. I want you to be who you are and what you are."

He hugged her and stepped up out of the water. Holding hands, they returned to their sheltered place. Lucy identified the twined trees. "Isn't that hawthorn?"

"May, we call it," he said.

"But it can't be in flower now. It blooms in October."

"*Over there*, maybe. My father brings it to Mammy when it's blooming there. But here, it flowers in this month and next, so we call it May."

Lucy lay down on the moss. A few white petals floated down to kiss her naked body. She held out her arms.

Paris kneeled beside her and kissed her mouth. It was warm and sweet, and then suddenly, his energy surged up, and she dragged him down and forgot everything but the sensation of being *treasured*.

She squealed until she was breathless and then squealed again as his joyful release broke over her in a wave.

Chapter Twenty-one: Lorelei Has Had Enough

August Herron, 2020, Ferris Island

It was three days since Paris had carried Lucy Tan out of the cottage on Ferris Island. August was getting worried.

"She can't get back if Paris won't bring her," he said to Lorelei as he placed a block of wood on its end.

"Now you're being silly. You know anyone would let her through the gate."

"But that seaman probably scares them off. He scares *me*."

"That willy of his is a sight to behold. No wonder that order has a fearsome reputation," Lorelei said.

"He wouldn't . . ."

"I'm sure he wouldn't. Even seamen must have some sense of decency, and *that* willy would need to be used with care, even on a woman it'll fit. August, stop worrying."

"Sooner or later someone will ask where they've got to."

"I doubt it. The companions know better, and the Mini-Mal-Lists are totally caught up in their own affairs." She added, "Augie, there's only so long I'm going to let you fret over this. No doubt you'll catch up with someone eventually and find out what's behind it all."

He brought his axe down on a piece of wood, remembering Lucy stacking for him the day after that embarrassing proposition.

I have to stop obsessing – Lorelei's right.

Great bogle, have I done the girl a favour or messed up her life for good?

He brought down the axe again, and it mis-hit, sending the wood skittering sideways.

Lorelei conjured it out of the way just in time.

"August Herron!" She jammed her hands on her hips. "I've had enough of this. We're going through that cave tonight, and then you're going to the Castle Bridge gate to call Jack Miller. I don't care if he's asleep or pruning the roses or cock-deep in the porridge pot. You get him down to the falls and we'll get things sorted once and for all."

CHAPTER TWENTY-TWO: CLOTHES

Lucy Tan, 2020, Over there

Lucy and Paris spent a magical three days together at the mossy glade. No one else came to disturb them, but Lucy was touched to see a huge basket of bread and cheese, cake and fruit appear out of nowhere soon after their trip to the cascade.

"Mama Tam," Paris said. He pointed to the bread. "That's Liam Dancey's soda loaf. I'd know it anywhere, and she's sent butter from Crock o' Gold. That's a leppy village where the colleens keep cows."

Lucy was already tearing a piece off the loaf. She hadn't realised how hungry she was.

"Better get some, before I eat it all," she mumbled. She indicated a squat, opaque bottle. "Zat poteen?"

Paris took the loaf and buttered some. "Cider. Liam would gift you poteen, but he'd want to be on hand to watch you drink it. He's proud of his baking and brewing."

She giggled. "Not on your life. Never again. It makes me say—" She choked.

It makes me say what I mean.

A glad realisation swept over her.

"No! I'd love some . . . because it won't make any difference at all!"

She laughed, and Paris grabbed her in his arms. They rolled over like puppies until the inevitable happened and Lucy was seeing stars.

On the third day, with the stores in the basket depleted, she reminded him that he'd offered to introduce her to his mother.

"She won't mind about me, will she?"

"Why would she? She wants me to be happy."

"I suppose she won't mind me being human. After all, your dad is."

Paris said nothing, but she felt the gentle fizz of his presence waver.

"About that," she said abruptly.

He turned his beautiful grey eyes to hers.

"I'm not an expert on genetics, but I did do high school science. Your mother is waterfolk, like Mama Tam, right?"

He nodded. "More traditional. Mama Tam wears clothes sometimes."

"*Half* wears clothes," Lucy said, remembering. "You did notice that freelance bosom, right?"

"I did. It's pretty, but I never play with Mama Tam."

"I know. She told me she was your *catcher*. Does that mean midwife? I mean, did she help your mother when she was giving birth?"

"That's what she does."

"Aside from having children with hand-picked fathers."

"How else?"

"I got the impression she raised a few eyebrows when she had her son Tane with a pisky man."

He shrugged.

"Your dad's human. Does that bother any of your people?"

He hesitated. "It's not usual, but it doesn't bother them. Why should it?"

"Why should it? Because there must have been an even chance you'd be—I mean you'd *present as* human. What would have happened?"

He looked away, and she felt him withdrawing.

"Would you have had to live with your dad?"

"Both places, I think. No one ever said."

"Does being with a human feel wrong to you? You have to make concessions to me. Give me water gift . . . and I can't conjure, obviously."

"You're lovely."

"Yes, I know. I'm lovely. I deserve happiness, and being with you lets me know that. You never expect or want me to be anything other than I am. I love you. I know you won't love me the way I think of it because you are what you are and soon, you'll go back to doing what you do. All those maids and lassies and ladies must be missing you. I suppose I should feel bad for them that I'm taking up all your time . . . but I don't. I love you, and this is my magical time. I *know* you can't love me. And that's all right."

She hadn't planned that declaration, and she had no idea how he'd react. She knew he wouldn't rush into protestations the way a human might, so she was barely disappointed when he said nothing.

"I love you because you're you," she said.

And that's why I've always loved Augie . . .

And why I love Otto.

She laughed, although tears prickled her eyes. "I love August Herron. You know that, right?"

He nodded. "Felt it."

"I have for years. I don't want him. I did once, but now I just love him. He makes my world happier. I used to think he was perfect, but then one day we had a picnic with some special cake. Courting cake. You know what that is?"

"Hobs make it," he said.

"Whatever was in it, it let me see what kind of love I had for him. Do you know, when I was young, I had the chance to be Queen of the May? I gave it up to be with him."

His face lit up. "There's a May Day Ball at the castle! You

could be my queen!"

"You — what?"

"The castle up in the courtlands. They hold midsummer balls, and Christmas dances, and New Year . . . and May Day."

"You go to *balls*?" She couldn't imagine it, although he was a beautiful mover.

"No . . . but the elf girls tell me about it. Anyone can go." He grabbed her hands, and she felt the sherbet and popcorn dancing.

"A *ball*? Don't you have to wear — um — clothes?"

He laughed, pulled her in and kissed her. "Yes . . . that's why my people don't go. We hear about it, though, and we have our own dances. If you want to go with me . . . I *can* wear clothes."

She glanced over to where their Camp Ferris clothing lay neatly folded under the tree.

"You don't like to, though."

She felt his withdrawal, but when he would have pulled back, she held him fast by the upper arms and pulled him down. "Paris, look at me. What is it with you and clothes? You made such a fuss about not wanting to wear anything. I see your point. You don't feel cold, and you are so beautiful. Why would you ever cover up your gorgeous body?" She let go of one arm and stroked his cock. "Even this. On most men, it's . . . well, not something I want to look at. On you, it's as beautiful as the rest of you. In fact, I want it in me now."

She had been kneeling, but she moved forward to straddle him. "Can you — of course, you can." She slipped into position and closed her eyes as delight ran through her.

"You love this, don't you? Even now when I'm making you listen to me babble." She squirmed until she had him seated more firmly. "That's lovely, but keep still. I haven't finished talking yet." She wrapped her arms and legs around him.

"Now, let's get this two-way feeling going on. Can you *feel* me?" She opened her mind, throwing out her uncertainties. "This is *me*. It's the me you helped make. I love you for that. I won't ever give up a chance I want again, so yes, I want to come to this May Day Ball with you. I'm going to get hold of a dress somehow . . . maybe one of your lovers would help? But you can go bare. I won't mind a bit." She leaned forward and kissed him slowly and moved against him. "No, you keep still. Is that good?" She laughed breathlessly. "It is! I can feel you loving it. Now . . . tell me, what *is* it with you and clothes?"

Paris squirmed, but Lucy had him where she wanted him. "You don't get to have your lovely stars and heaven moment until you tell me . . . and neither do I. And I *want* it. Can't you feel how much I want it? So *tell me*."

He moaned, and then he told her.

Lucy gasped, laughed and thrust herself against him, feeling the first warning flutters. "Oh, you silly sausage! You *silly* sausage!"

She was still laughing uproariously when the fireworks went up.

CHAPTER TWENTY-THREE: THE HAIRY HIGHLANDER

Lucy Tan, 2020, Over there

Lucy and Paris arrived at the falls just in time to see a red-haired woman fling herself on a tall bearded man wearing a kilt and hurl them both into the water.

"That's my mammy," Paris said as the pair surfaced.

The man in the kilt was roaring like a bull elephant.

"But that's not Mister Miller." Lucy glanced about where more waterfolk than she'd seen before swam, cuddled and picnicked by the wide pool. Some of them were watching the spectacle and smiling.

She narrowed her eyes, feeling *déjà vu.*

I wonder if Gran Qin ever brought me here when I was little? If she did, no wonder Mum disapproved. All this freelance love –

"That's Cameron Dougal from the brae. He's been coming to Mammy since I was a tiddler. We'd better wait until they're finished."

Lucy watched with slightly horrified amusement as the kilted man scrambled out of the large pool, displaying a broad expanse of hairy arse, and turned to face the water.

"Oot here, wumman, noo! I'll no' swelp ye in yon water!" he roared, in such a broad accent Lucy could barely understand him. "Ye'll gae to it on drei land like a Christian."

The redhead leaned her folded arms on the rock and put her chin on them.

"Make me," she taunted.

"Oot ye coom!" The man bent and hauled her out.

Lucy gasped as the kilt rode up, giving her a fine view of hairy balls.

That's a sight I'll never unsee . . .

Crowing with success, the hairy highlander carried the redhead up the grassy slope to where a woollen blanket lay spread out. He flopped down, lay on his back, and lifted the kilt, displaying more of his person.

The woman yelled and sat down on him, yelling again when he roared, and then bursting into musical laughter.

It was all noisy and vigorous, and Lucy found she couldn't look away.

When it was over, the woman got up and stretched, lithe as a cat. The man arched his back and propelled himself to his feet, with the kilt flopping down to cover him to his muscular calves.

"Aye, lassie, ye still have the touch an' still got yon magical coochie."

She laughed, shaking back her hair. It dried immediately. She turned slowly.

A flash of delight lit her pert features, and she ran down the slope, breasts jiggling merrily. "Paris, lovely! You didn't stay in that place, then?"

Paris hugged her. "I tried, Mammy."

"But you—"

The highlander arrived in a few giant strides. He grinned at Paris. "Your mammy's in fine form today, laddie. Never squirted me so fast. And I see ye've business yoursel', so I willnae keep you." He gave Paris a one-armed hug and winked at Lucy over his shoulder. "This young cockie will do ye proud. Wish I cuid say he was *my* get but—" He brightened. "Mind, I got a fine laddie on Fiona Mackie. She was sae wantin' to plant a bairn she said she'd overlook the hairy arse and bollocks." He seemed about to say more, but his attention turned to the path behind them. He raised a hand and roared,

"Jack, mun! Come and drink a dram wi' me when ye can tear yerself away from this wumman!"

"I'll do that, Cam. Good to see you."

Lucy turned and felt her eyes bug as she beheld the three people approaching.

Oh. My. God.

Being bare among the waterfolk was fine. None of them appeared to notice . . . except for Paris. He liked to look at her, but she supposed that was to do with his ability to *feel* what she liked. He was unerring in that. If she wanted to cuddle, he cuddled. If she wanted to *fuck like bunnies,* he was hard and vigorous. The highlander kept his friendly gaze on her face after his first once-over. She could hardly object since she'd seen rather a lot of him.

Being bare in front of Mister Miller, the groundsman from her old school, was another matter.

Being bare in front of his companions was far worse. She cringed.

Chapter Twenty-four: Unbelievable

Lucy Tan, 2020, Over there

Paris must have noticed her embarrassment. "Want your clothes, my Lucy?"

Yes.

"A bit late now," she said.

"You're lovely, all bare. You'll be lovely when we have you gowned for the May Day Ball."

Oh. My. Lord.

She manufactured a smile. "Hello, Mister Miller. Lorelei. Augie."

She caught a flash of dismay in August's eyes, but Lorelei smiled and came over to stand beside her. "Hello, Lucy. I see you feel better now."

"Um . . . yes." Lucy lifted her chin, leaned over and whispered, "We took your advice and fucked like bunnies. We're still doing it."

Lorelei giggled. "That's wonderful. Nothing like it, is there?"

"What are you doing here?" Lucy asked, but she failed to hear the answer because she saw Paris hugging his father.

She hadn't seen Jack Miller in eight years, but now she saw how much like Paris he was.

The hug was necessarily a brief one, because Fee pushed between them and raised her face to kiss Jack with great enthusiasm.

He hugged her back and murmured something in her ear,

which made her laugh.

The highlander looked on wistfully.

"I offered that wumman my plaidie and balls on a plate, but she sets her cap at yon red streak o' a human. No accounting for wummen."

"I'm human," Lucy pointed out.

The man turned his attention to her, and she saw with interest that his eyes were changing colour in an endless cycle of lavender, blue and aqua. "Right bonnie, too, lassie. Seeing ye bare made me think ye must be water. Reckon ye're here for more than a play with the fine cockie, then."

He flicked his hand upwards in a curious motion and was suddenly holding a set of bagpipes, which he depressed with a mournful wail. He raised the blowstick to his lips and set off, marching in time to his tune.

"That's *Road to the Isles*," Lucy said, surprised.

"There was a lot of cultural exchange here at one time," Lorelei said.

Paris stepped back, and Lucy watched Jack Miller and Fee, who appeared to be having a wrestling match on the lip of the pool. The man was taller and broader than the lithe water maid, but Lucy saw the affair was going to go the woman's way.

Splash.

Yes, there they went, sinking into the water. Fee's lips were on Jack's, and Lucy supposed she was giving him what Paris called *water gift*.

"Fee told me there's a chamber below the falls. They'll probably be a while," Lorelei said. She reached over and prodded her husband in the ribs. "August, aren't you going to say anything to Lucy?"

He glanced at Lucy and then away, and she saw dull red on his cheeks.

He's embarrassed?

She backed against Paris, and his warm arms came around

her.

He's dialled down again — my lovely Paris.

She bent forward a little and rubbed against him. "Real you, remember?" Then she said, "Augie?"

He was still looking away.

"What's wrong with him? He's a counsellor," she said to Lorelei.

"He's also an elf man who *lives human*," Lorelei said in a dry voice. "As for exactly what's bugging him now, I don't quite know. It can't be just seeing his pet ex-student in a state of delightful nature. It's something deeper. That's what I dragged him here to find out." She looked Lucy up and down. "You really are blooming, my girl. Is Paris as good a lover as you expected?"

"I wasn't expecting anything. You pushed the issue with your intervention. If that's what it was."

"I know. I don't usually stick my nose into other people's business. That's August's role, not mine. But it was as plain as the nose on that hairy highlander's face that you two were glitching. There were sparks between you, and they were being put out as fast as they lit. It set my teeth on edge. I'm very angry with August for the situation he put you in, and I think I'm going to be angrier when we get this sorted out."

Lucy remembered a time, not so long ago, where she would have had ambiguous feelings about a rift between August Herron and the love of his life. It seemed unreal and far away.

"I hope not," she said.

She wriggled her shoulder blades against Paris's chest, and he slipped up a hand to cup her breast. "Are you two going to take your clothes off?" she asked Lorelei.

"I doubt it." She turned back to her husband. "August, will you stop doing that? You're making poor Lucy uncomfortable. *Not* looking at her is far worse than looking, believe me, and I don't think she ought to have to get dressed just to please you. Just have a look, and get over it."

August turned his gaze on her at last and winced away.

"What the hell's wrong? You wanted this to happen, didn't you?" Lucy said. She peeled herself away from Paris and stepped up to confront her old teacher. "Paris and I have worked out some of this godawful scheme, we think, but you and his dad will have to fill in the blanks." She turned to Paris. "The suspense is getting to me, and Augie's about to go into meltdown. Will it be too embarrassing for you to dive down and drag your parents out of whatever they're doing?"

"Will you be all right if I go?"

"I will *always* be all right—now." She gave him a quick hug and kiss and watched him dive into the pool.

Lorelei said, "You really are all right, aren't you, Lucy?"

"Yes. I'm who I am and where I want to be." She grinned and put her hand on her old teacher's arm. "Unbelievable! Augie, did you ever think, way back when, that we'd be standing here in fairyland, with you and the love of your life in nineteenth-century costume and me in the altogether, waiting for two fairies and a human groundsman to come out of a pool?"

August seemed to relax a little at last.

"I think you can safely take that as a no, dear Lucy."

The waiting went on . . . and on.

Lucy went up the grassy slope to Fee's plaid blanket and said, "Is that safe to sit on?"

Lorelei came up behind her. "Perfectly. It's braeside wool, which repels dirt, and you probably know you can't catch anything from any of us."

"Except a baby," Augie said darkly.

"But only if it's intentional . . . right?"

To her fascination, Augie and Lorelei exchanged rueful glances.

"What?"

"I'll explain to you later," Lorelei said.

Okaaaay.

They sat on the blanket and waited some more.

"What are they doing?" Lorelei asked irritably.

"Probably getting their stories straight. I think I might tell you the bit I know, to fill in the time."

Two faces turned to her. Lorelei looked expectant. August looked nervous.

"Before you two showed up on the island, I took Paris to the stores to get him some clothes," Lucy said.

"That must have been fun," Lorelei said.

"He resisted the whole concept of clothing."

"They do, mostly."

"But he's not a *they*. He's almost as much human as he is waterfolk, and I think the reason he *presents* as waterfolk is because he lives like one."

"Physically, I'd say he's close to pure," Lorelei said.

"Maybe, but didn't you see him with Mister Miller? They're both tall, and they both stand the same way. Their voices even sound similar. I can't remember Mister Miller saying anything much more than *good morning* when I was at school, except for one time when we talked about a tree. But then he just called out to that hairy highlander . . . or whatever he was, and his voice was familiar. It's because he sounds like Paris."

"Your highlander is a braeside laddie," Augie said.

"*Laddie*? He's got to be fifty!"

"A braeman is a laddie from birth until death. We elves use the girl, boy, man, woman terms . . . although if I lived *over here*, I'd probably be styled as an *elf maid*," Lorelei said.

"Anyway, when I was explaining about the clothing, he wouldn't even *look* at it. I had to get sharp to get him to put some on. I chose a green shirt because he's got red hair, but he suddenly took an interest and picked out a blue one."

"But they don't do that," Augie said.

"I'm just telling you, he's not a *they*. Then he wouldn't look at himself, and then when he did, he thought I wanted him in green. I said he should please himself, and then he picked cream, I think because it matched the one I had on. He looks good in it. The point is, once I got him to pay attention, he was interested in clothes all right."

"That's odd, but what has it to do with this mess?" Lorelei asked.

"He's been skittery about the subject all through, but I finally got him pinned down and pried it out of him. He was *ashamed*."

"But they don't—"

Lucy turned on her first love. "Augie, if you don't stop that, I'm going to kick you where it hurts. Paris is not a *they*. His people here are a certain way because they like to be that way and because they learn it from their mothers. I accept they can't handle the air and water in Sydney, say, and I accept they need lots of physical attention, and to be near and about water. It's perfectly clear they have amazing lungs and water-resistant skin. They are beautiful and much more . . . well, foreign . . . than any fay I'd met before. Not that I'd met many . . .

"But Paris is half-human, so that side of him is more like me than like you, even. I don't know Mister Miller's human family, but I bet there's someone in it who loves clothes and pretty things. Whether it's an aunt who collects vintage fabrics or a great-granny who makes her own hats, or a sister who knits Doctor Who scarves for cos-play, there's someone in the Miller family who has a love affair with fabrics.

"Paris loves the feel of cloth. He's intrigued by it, but he's embarrassed about it because he thinks it marks him apart from . . . his friend London, maybe. And I'm going to make sure he knows that it's *all right* to love something his folk here don't care about." She leaned back on her hands. "Lorelei, when summer comes, am I going to have to wear sunscreen *over here* to avoid getting burned?"

"Great bogle . . ."

She shot a glare at August.

"*Yes,* I am going to keep coming here. Now that I've found my beautiful Paris, I'm going to come to him and *fuck like bunnies* whenever I feel the urge. I expect I'll feel it a lot. In between, he can go on doing what he does with his maids and lassies. I'll go on companioning with Vouch-Safe, but I'm not losing this chance to be with my perfect man. Right? I'm having it both ways, and so is he."

August put his face in his hands.

For a few moments, Lucy thought he was crying, but then she realised he was laughing. His shoulders shook.

"Is he all right?" she asked Lorelei.

"I expect so. He hasn't really been the same since I fucked him silly and then wrapped his willy in a frozen cloth."

"You–what?"

"*No harm.* Our kind doesn't get frostbite."

"But *why? Why* would you do that to him?"

Lorelei said, "The medical answer is something to do with stimulating circulation. I applied a hot compress, and then an iced one, and then I scrubbed him up with a rough towel. He went a pretty rose pink, so it must have worked."

"Bullshit. You just wanted to torture him." Lucy achieved a fiendish grin. "That's how I got Paris to man up and tell me his not-so-shameful secret."

"You tortured a water lad with a frozen cloth?"

"No, but I put him in a spot and blackmailed him. Sort of. He let me do it because he felt I wanted to."

"I'm sure he enjoyed it. I'm not so sure about Augie."

"I was thinking, just before Paris came out of the cave on Ferris and scared the shit out of me, that I should find myself an elf man to call my own. I've been with humans, but the only men I ever loved were both elves. But now I've found out what I really needed all along."

They sat and watched August wrestle with whatever it was, and after a bit, Lorelei put her arm around Lucy in sisterly solidarity. "Lucy, my love, men are a pain in the arse. A bit of torturing is what they need to put them in their places. Anyway, he got me back with an ice cube. I trust whatever your Paris does to you in revenge will be equally delightful." She sighed loudly and then looked up. "Oh, here they come. Finally."

Chapter Twenty-five: Jack Miller's Wish

Lucy Tan, 2020, Over there

The red-headed Fee had her man and her son by the hands, and she was talking volubly. Paris detached himself and strode ahead to sit by Lucy.

"Sorry about that. It took a while to get Mammy to listen."

The other two came up, and Jack Miller lowered himself cautiously to the blanket. Fee plopped herself in his lap and Lucy breathed a silent prayer of thanks. She had learned to filter out the swinging bits and bobs on the waterfolk, but Jack Miller was a middle-aged human, and besides, he was *Mister Miller*, from school.

He saw her looking and gave her a shy smile. "Lucy. My son's been telling me I've inadvertently caused you some angst. I didn't mean to. I guess I didn't think it through."

"Do you remember me from school?" Lucy asked.

"Yes, you were one of the pleasant girls who used to smile at me and say *good morning*. I appreciated that. I remember you coming in to school on a Saturday, too. I was appropriating hawthorn flowers for Fee, but you didn't ask me what I thought I was doing. I thought you looked happy."

"I was. I was going to see Mister Herron."

"And now you work for the Vouch-Safe company."

"Yes, indirectly. I'm not a driver. I'm strictly a camp companion."

Fee jiggled impatiently. "Paris, lovely, aren't you going to — "

Paris said, "Lucy, this is my mammy. Fee. Mammy, this is Lucy."

Fee grinned impishly. She must have been well into her forties, but she exuded *joie de vivre*. "Greet you, darling."

"Settle down, Fee, and stop bouncing on my bits. I'm trying to explain our plan," Jack Miller said calmly.

He went on, "Lucy, Fee and I don't have a conventional marriage. Most waterfolk don't marry at all, but we got a fay priest to *say the words* for us. I love her dearly, and I'm faithful to her, but that's because I choose to be. She loves me in her fashion."

"Darling Jack, you're my favourite snuggler," Fee put in.

"Fee cares for the needs of fay men like Cam Dougal because that's what she does. I'm comfortable with that. My best friends . . . maybe my only real friends, are men who come and play with Fee. We have plenty in common, after all, and sometimes we share an ale and some courting cake. I know it's odd from the human perspective, but I am odd. I've always been odd. That's why I never settled down with a human woman."

"You didn't tell me you were wed," August said.

"There was a lot I didn't tell you, Master Herron.

"Fee is my love and a big part of my life. She's my joy, but I can't live here all the time. Paris is our son, and he was planned, and wanted, and loved. Fee wanted a baby, and she did *me* the honour of choosing me to help her make one. That's the reason I asked her to marry me."

Fee said, more calmly, "I'm a bit flighty, lovely. I wanted gentle blood for my babby."

"And so we *made* Paris. That's the way Fee puts it. We crafted him. Fee had me in water, which is natural for her, and then I had her under her braeside blanket, which is natural for me."

"Then he squealed me again, for fun," Fee said brightly.

"Fee said we'd planted him, and we planned to be a real family, with our child knowing both our worlds. But then Paris was born, and even though I made it here just in time to lift him out of the pool and welcome him, he grew up *throwing hard* to water. I was sorry he couldn't do things with me *over there,* but he's the best son a man ever had."

"I'm sure he is," Lucy said. She had no idea where this was going.

"So Paris got man grown and set up in the same vocation as Fee, though he doesn't throw maids into the water and jump in with them. Fee and I thought he was set the way he'd go on, and we both hoped sometime one of the women he tends to might choose to make us a grandchild. But then a few things changed."

Fee leaned forward. "London and Kin made Lara."

Lucy said, "I met them. Kin told me she and London are a couple. Well, that's what she meant."

Fee nodded vigorously. "They sleep together, cuddly, same as darling Jack and me."

"Paris lost his best friend's attention."

"I'm happy for them," Paris protested.

Jack went on, "And since he wasn't always with London, I saw more of him, and I started to notice he had preferences I hadn't seen before."

"He was cold, too," Fee said.

"He started seeming more like me, and although that pleased me in a way, I saw that maybe Fee and I had made a mistake."

"No!" Fee protested.

"Not in making Paris, but in accepting he was waterfolk and that was that. And so I decided to talk things over with someone who might have an objective view." He nodded across to Augie. "Master Herron, that is. I'd known him a long time, though never well. I know he helps folk with problems to decide what to do. He's fay, so I thought he'd understand about waterfolk, and he's a husband and a father, so I thought he'd understand that we'll do *anything* for our son's happiness."

August cleared his throat. "That may be so, but it wasn't only an objective view you wanted, Jack. You really put me on the spot."

"You could have said no."

"To what?" Paris asked. He tucked his arms more firmly around Lucy, and she felt his anxiety. Instead of giving comfort and warmth, he was seeking it.

She reached up and put her arm around him, rubbing her cheek on his. Then she said, "Mister Miller, you're talking to other people about Paris. Why the fuck didn't you talk to him? He's not a kid."

Jack turned to gaze at her with compassion. "I know, Lucy. I tried that."

Paris nodded against Lucy's hair. "He did. I didn't want to listen."

"And that's another clue that our Paris isn't your typical waterfolk person."

"*In denial* is the way we put it in the counselling business," August said.

"So I came up with something you might accept," Jack said to Paris.

"Camp Ferris," August said.

"And I slanted it to suggest I wanted it for my benefit, to spend more time with you. I knew you'd try for me. It was probably unforgivable."

Jack looked unhappy, and again Lucy was struck to his likeness to his son. Fee leaned her head on his bare shoulder. "You wanted to make him happy," she said.

"I did. I do. But I think I always knew you can't *make* some-one happy." Jack was speaking to Paris again. "I should have left you alone, to find your own way, my son. I can imagine how I'd have felt if your grandpa Miller had tried to make *me* change my ways."

"You still haven't told Paris what you actually did," Lucy said.

"He did tell me some of it. He told me in the under cave," Paris informed her.

"Are you going to tell me? It doesn't matter if you're not."

"We're going to tell you because you have a right to know," Augie said.

Jack nodded. "I put the situation to Master Herron. I told him what I'd talked over with Paris, and then I told him the rest of it and what I wanted him to do. He didn't want to do it."

"I did not," August said grimly.

"So I played an underhand card . . . and made a wish," Jack continued.

"Great bogle! August Herron . . . you didn't!" Lorelei ex-claimed.

"I didn't intend to." August said to Lucy, "I doubt if you know about wishes, Lucy, but some fay can service them. They have to be specific and possible, and they have to be eth-ically sound. Do you understand?"

She nodded, dazed. "My grandmother used to tell me wish stories. Mister Miller, what did you wish for?"

"I wished, clearly and specifically, that Master Herron would find a way for my son to reconcile with both sides of his nature. I couldn't wish the human side gone, because if it was lost, Paris wouldn't be who he is. I hoped that being with humans and with no distractions might help him to recognise the human parts in himself and not see them as flaws."

"The clothes," Lucy said.

Jack looked uncomprehending, and she remembered he hadn't been there when she'd told Augie and Lorelei about the clothing. She explained it again, briefly.

Jack nodded. "Paris, you know I choose to go bare when I come home to you and Fee. It was never meant to say *you* must always go bare. It simply never occurred to me you might want to wear clothing."

"I don't," Paris said quickly.

Lucy said, "Paris and I are going to the May Day Ball at the castle. I am going to wear a dress if I can get one. *He* is going in his beautiful skin."

Lorelei gasped and choked, subsiding in a coughing fit.

Augie patted her anxiously on the back.

Jack's naturally pale skin turned a greenish hue, and he looked unwell.

Fee nodded cheerfully. "I want to go, too! Mistress Herron? You like to dance?"

"Great bogle!" Augie's face suffused with a dark blush. "Jack, she *can't*."

Jack gulped audibly and put a possessive hand on his lover's breast. "She can so! Fee, darling, if you want to go, we'll go. And if anyone dares to lift a courtly eyebrow, I'll remind the assembly that a great many of the men are obliged to you for your expert attentions, and many of the ladies are obliged to you for teaching their men to be fun in bed."

Augie looked as if he was going to be sick.

Fee looked at him compassionately. "Master Herron, will it make you feel better if I get Mama Tam to ask her man to have his sister make a gown for me?"

Augie said tightly, "Mistress, I would never ask that of you."

Fee cocked her head against Jack's shoulder. "You want to give me something pretty? You like to see me in a gown?"

"Only because I'll know about the beauty it conceals," he

said, laughing.

"Oh, so will everyone else," Fee said smugly. She looked at Lucy. "It will be fun. You can be pretty, too. Make sure you have Paris before you go. Otherwise, his cock will get—"

Jack put his hand over Fee's mouth.

Paris sighed. "Mammy, you're naughty. I might wear clothes if Lucy wants it."

"I will be equally happy whatever you decide," Lucy said.

August looked at her with an odd expression.

"What?"

"You mean that, don't you?"

"Yes, of course. I assume it's not an actual offence to go to a ball in your skin?"

"There are not too many offences *over here*."

"And there's the way my wish worked out," Jack said quietly. "Master Herron made it possible for Paris to be with humans in a place where he would be able to breathe without pain. He also made it as comfortable as possible for him, by making sure there would be no one he would feel the need to *comfort*."

"But unfortunately, Paris really does need hands-on affection, so—"

"So I was the sacrificial lamb," Lucy said, without heat.

"August Herron!" Lorelei's voice snapped dangerously.

Augie cringed.

Lucy considered letting him suffer, but then she remembered she loved him still. "It's okay, Augie. You were trying to keep him safe, and you warned me to be specific. I had a chance to say no."

"I did try, and I thought it was all right," Paris said.

Jack said quietly, "It *is* all right, my son. Lucy is one of those rare souls who loves and is happy in her love. I know, because I'm one, too."

Lucy smiled. "That's what I've decided," she said to Jack.

"I can be Paris's human love, and I'll love him forever. I can come to him here the way you come to Fee. It won't make any difference to what he does for his maids and lassies, because I'm the one who gets to love him. Does that make sense?"

Jack's grey eyes, so like his son's, crinkled with amusement. "Lucy, I'd take my hat off to you if I was wearing one. That's the way I feel about Fee."

"Love you, too, my darling Jack," Fee said.

"I know you do. But you're fine when I can't be here, right?"

"Of course," she agreed, giggling. "You know why?"

"Because you have Cam Dougal and plenty of other upstanding fay men to keep you entertained," he said dryly.

Fee snuggled against him like a kitten. She looked across at Lucy, and Lucy saw the soul behind her eyes.

"Tell him, Fee. Why *are* you happy when Mister Miller is working *over there*?" she said.

"It's because I know he'll come back, and we'll sleep under our blanket again," Fee said.

Chapter Twenty-six: A Bug in Spider Silk

August Herron, 2020, Ferris Island

August sat on his bed in the cottage on Ferris Island. He wanted to rock himself for comfort, but he resisted the urge.

He did not look at his wife, who was putting on her nightdress, slowly, in the human way for once. He foresaw his next Christmas Hot would be unbearable.

Stiff as a poker and nowhere to stick it.

That was nothing, really. It was the implication of abandonment that terrified him.

The Christmas Hot was something of a joke among non-elves, but no elf would joke about it. It turned grown, self-assured fairy men into whimpering messes desperate for affection.

It gave him an unpleasant insight into the way waterfolk presumably felt if deprived of the two-way stream of physical affection. They had to give as well as receive, he knew. For many, any warm and willing maid or man would do, but Paris was oriented towards females.

Hence his co-opting of the calm and steadfast Lucy Tan.

"Come to bed, Augie." Lorelei's voice interrupted his misery.

"I'd better check on—"

"August Herron. Now."

He conjured off his outer clothing and got into bed.

The love of his life clicked her fingers, dousing the lantern light. In the darkness of the cottage, she turned towards him and rolled him into her arms, with his head pillowed on her breasts.

"That was an interesting interlude," she said.

There was no sarcasm in her tone.

"Are you sure Jack Miller's great-grandfather wasn't a pisky?"

"Leprechaun, he said. Paddy Shillelagh."

"I suppose he'd know, but I wouldn't have said leprechaun blood would make him so manipulative. That fancy footwork has pisky all over it."

"You're overlooking the human quotient," he said.

"Huh." She shrugged, making him aware of her soft flesh under the cambric.

"He got you wrapped up like a bug in spider silk."

"I allowed it."

"I imagine it was difficult to resist. He's a powerful personality."

"Jack Miller?"

"Oh, yes. Have you any idea what he did before he was a groundsman?"

"No, only that he lost that job because he met Fee and fell in love with her." He dared to roll his face a little, seeking the gap between the ties. "Did you know he steals the school's flowers to take to Fee?"

She laughed. "Doesn't he grow them?"

"Yes."

"There you are, then."

"He's so quiet at work. Diffident."

"Dialled down. Clearly, humans can do it, too," she said.

Augie's nose found the gap.

Lorelei conjured off her nightgown and his drawers.

He nuzzled gratefully and trapped a nipple between his lips.

"You can do better than that," she taunted.

He pressed against her.

It was a good long while until Christmas, but he was confident of generating heat.

Chapter Twenty-seven: May Day

Lucy Tan, 2020, Ferris Island and Over there

Lucy got out of bed while the last of the starlight still greyed the cottage window. She put on her skirt and blouse, rolled on her stockings and slipped into her boots.

Then she stepped back to the bed.

"Paris?" She put a hand on her lover's bare shoulder.

He was instantly awake, sitting up almost before he opened his eyes.

He held out his arms, and she perched on the bed to hug him. Warmth poured back to her, but no popcorn. Considering they'd been awake and active half the night it was little wonder he was settled to a sweet simmer.

"Why are you dressed, my Lucy?"

"Because this is Ferris Island, and here, we wear clothes."

"Hmph." He grumbled a bit but got out of bed. With a flick of his fingers against his cheek, he was clad in pants and a shirt. "Where are we going?"

"I want to show you something. August showed it to me once, but I've never managed to get there at just the right time again."

He took her hand, and they left the cottage, heading for the water caves.

The sun hadn't lifted when they arrived, and Lucy perched on the brim of the rock. "Are you going in?"

"Are you?"

"It's too cold for me, but you won't even notice."

He sat down beside her. "I'll stay with you."

Lucy leaned into him. "Paris, you said once your dad brought you books and sang you songs. What books were they?"

"All sorts. My favourites were the *Bitternut* books."

"Really? The ones by Jonathan Blarney? I have those, too. There was a bit of a fuss a few years back because the people in the paintings aren't always wearing clothes. He was clever with ferns and water and blowing hair though, so they weren't pulled from sale after all." Lucy recalled the delicate watercolours of meadows and caves, flowers, birds, trees and a laughing woman with red hair. There were small boys, too, one black and one with dark red hair. The redhead had been standing on his dad's shoulders in one spread. She caught her breath and laughed. *Déjà vu!* No wonder!

Paris kissed her hair.

"Your dad wrote those and drew the pictures, didn't he? You were in them, and your mum, and London, and Mama Tam, with her sarong on properly." It wasn't a question.

"My father brings his paints to us at the falls. That's why I like the books," Paris said. He stretched out a foot and splashed it in the water, just as the sun rose, sending its gold and diamonds to light up the water.

Paris slid into the pool and held out his arms to Lucy.

She went to him. It was cold, but he'd have her warm and dry in no time.

After breakfast, *Robinson Crusoe* arrived, blue sails glowing against the crisp autumn skies.

Unlike most campers, the Mini-Mal-Lists had no problem with the concept of taking nothing with them. They made efficient work of the last round of animal chores and dressed obediently in the generic clothing in which they'd arrived. They washed their camp clothing and pegged it out to dry, and then, talking quietly, they made for the ship.

"You're not coming with us?" one of the men asked, noting Lucy was still in camp clothes.

"Someone has to be here to look after the animals. We always have a skeleton staff of companions here."

"Well . . . it's been a treat, Lois. Nev and I nearly didn't come, what with the short notice, but we've loved our time here." He took her hand. "I know protocol says we'll never see you again, but could you answer me a question?"

"That depends," she said warily.

"Just this. Do you ever have vacancies for companions? And if so, where should we direct our application?"

Lucy saw no harm in answering that one. "There are no vacancies for Camp Ferris, but there are new camps out there. Not many, because we like to keep things exclusive, and finding suitably isolated venues that can be reached in a reasonable time isn't easy. The Vouch-Safe company is the head office. I can't recommend you, because of the camp policy, but you can apply on your own recognisance. If you're successful, I might see you again."

"Thank you, Lois." He smiled and turned away.

Lucy realised she didn't even know his name.

I've been too distracted with Paris and all.

She'd been surprised when Paris elected to return and see the camp out. He'd moved into her cottage without discussion, but she still wasn't sure if it was to fend off soul cold or whether he just wanted to be with her. She could ask, but why put him on the spot with a question he might be unwilling, or unable, to answer?

As *Robinson Crusoe* sailed out into open water, she turned to him and asked a simpler question. "Are you going back home now?"

"You're coming with me."

"I am?"

"It's May Day. We're going to the ball."

"We all are," August said from where he was leaning on the jetty rail. He sounded relaxed and happy, and Lucy smiled at him with affection.

"Will you save me a dance, Master Herron?"

"He will if Paris will save me one," Lorelei said.

"I thought you didn't like to get turned on in public?"

"I don't, so I trust you'll see to defusing him beforehand."

"I can do that."

"I've been thinking about gowns," Lorelei said.

"I'll try to borrow something from one of Paris's lovers."

"I'm popping out through the Castle Bridge gate to get one from home. Would you like me to bring you something?"

"I'd fall over the hem," Lucy said, grinning at the thought. "Not being a tall and willowy elf maiden."

"Listen to your doctor. You're a perfectly proportioned young woman," Lorelei said. She mimed using a set square. "The courtfolk genes don't hurt. They give you beautiful carriage. The gown I have in mind is tea-length on me, so it should be about the same as your camp skirts on you. I had it made by an alpenfee dressmaker before Bethlehem was born, and I think it would be perfect on you."

"Thank you!"

"Thank *you*, Lucy, dear." She took Lucy's hands. "I don't ever poke my nose into other folks' business, but if you ever need a friend or a sounding board about anything concerning loving a fairy man, I'll be happy to step in. As I said, men are a pain in the arse, and I expect fairy men are worse than most."

"I *am* here," August said from her other side.

"I know you are. I can feel you looking at my neck with amorous intent. Lucy, love, I'll give you my email address and my mobile number. Hear that, August? If Lucy calls and you answer my phone, she wants to talk to *me*. Give her your number, and if she wants to talk to *you*, she can ring that."

At one time having Mister Herron's personal number would

have been heaven . . .

August dropped a kiss on his wife's neck and said to Paris, "Let's run a check on the livestock before we leave."

Left with Lorelei, Lucy thought about phones and computers and shops and commuter trains. And then she thought of the mossy may tree shelter and the cascade and the falls and the cliffs and the pixie forest which she wanted to explore.

Lorelei said, "You need to go back to Sydney, my dear. It's your world, just as it's mine. We are the way we're made. I've *lived human* all my life. I was born in Sydney, and my work is there. Nevertheless, I have to go *over there* at times, to reconnect with what I am. I went to the falls for my first experience of sex. So did Augie. We hadn't met at that time. We've been taking the girls through the gate since they were babies. When they *have enough years,* as they say *over there,* they can choose the way they want to live. They'll be fine, either way."

"Is that a gentle warning?"

"I suppose so. You're mostly human, and you need to express yourself in those terms. Jack Miller certainly does. He's devoted to that mad water maid of his, but he knows better than to live at the falls full-time."

Lucy hesitated and then took the plunge. "If Paris and I ever decide to *make a babby,* what will happen?"

"Heavens, you do choose awkward questions. I could be obtuse and say, well, you'll have a baby. I think you're asking a bit more than that, though."

"Yes, I'm asking you as a doctor. Would you rather I came to your surgery and made an appointment?"

"I have more patients than I know what to do with! What's your concern?"

"If I had Paris's baby, he . . . or she . . . would be almost three-quarters human."

Lorelei nodded. "Oh, I see. You're asking me for a genetic forecast. I can't give you an accurate answer. He or she could throw one way or the other, or maybe have strong attributes of both. That would be the rarer outcome, though. Look at Paris. Water halflings are comparatively rare, and so are water quarterlings, obviously. I'm out of the loop since I *live human*, but I really know only two—your Paris and Tane Pendennis. In both cases, they are the product of a water maid mother and a non-water dad, so they were both raised at the falls."

"Mama Tam told me she has several children, and she didn't mention any with a water lad."

"Mama Tam is not your usual water maid. Nevertheless, her children's fathers were all local men, who are no doubt proud and happy to have Tam and her children in their family circles. I'm certain she never handed any man a baby and said, *This one's yours so get on with it.*

"Your case would be different. I don't think you could bring up a child of Paris's entirely *over here.* Not only might it not thrive in the human world, but Paris would fret. Waterfolk bond strongly with their children. The parent-child bond seems to be their strongest imperative."

"After sex," Lucy remarked wryly.

"One imperative leads to the other. It's said waterfolk *always* know who fathers their children, and it's the maids who make the choice. They have only one or two children, so Tam is unusual in that way, too."

Lucy sighed.

"You should probably just ask Paris for his perspective," Lorelei said.

"I will, if the point ever comes up, but I don't want to ask him something and have him give me the answer he thinks I want."

"I think it probably will come up, since you've already thought of it. August and I were married for a while before we planted Bethlehem, but that was mostly because I had a heavy study load."

"You did the whole medical student thing?"

"Of course, I did! What did you think . . . that I snapped my fingers and glamoured up a diploma?"

"No."

"I could have, but since most of my patients are human, I owed it to them to tread the human road. August's teaching and counselling qualifications are genuine, too. It wasn't easy to juggle our lives, but we wanted to have children. Fortunately, we have relatives to help. Our girls are with their great-grandparents right now."

"I don't know what my parents would say . . ."

"You might ask them."

"So I might, but their opinion wouldn't sway me."

Just one more thing to consider.

I could have a baby with someone else. Paris wouldn't mind.

The other man probably would mind about Paris. I'm not giving up Paris. Or the chance to have a baby. I will have both.

Lucy pulled herself together.

"Lorelei, I don't know what I'll do, but I have decided I'm never going to give up a chance I want to have. If I want a baby with Paris, and if he wants it, too, then we'll find a way to make it work."

"It's early days yet," Lorelei said.

"Says the woman who *knew* as soon as she set eyes on a certain annoying elf man."

"Now, how do you happen to know about that?"

"August told me years ago. I offered him a cuddle, and he bolted. And then he took me for a walk and told me about *the love of his life.* Up until then, I'd assumed he was single."

Lorelei giggled. "Poor Augie. How he does hate it when people escape from the roles he's assigned to them. Fortunately, *love of his life* is a role I'm happy to occupy."

When the men came back, they all left the island. The tide was in, so August elected to use the trapdoor which debouched into the cave above water-level.

Lorelei opened the gateway, which Lucy couldn't see at all, and they stepped into the beautiful cave *over there*. Once on the chalk cliffs, they split up, with Paris and Lucy heading for the falls and August and Lorelei for the Castle Bridge gate.

"They'll be back in Sydney long before *Robinson Crusoe* makes it to port," Lucy said. She'd worn her island clothing, since she intended to return to caretake the livestock until the ship arrived with a new shift of campers and companions.

"Can we stop at our may tree place?" she asked.

"If you like." Paris hugged her against his side. He was bare, and Lucy noticed afresh how gracefully he moved.

At the may tree place, she found the twined trees in full bloom, frothing with pink and white. The sweet, soapy scent made her sneeze, but she took off her clothes and lay down on the moss.

Paris kneeled beside her and kissed her belly. Lucy squirmed as desire hit her.

"Lorelei says I have to defuse you before the ball," she said.

"Does that mean we *fuck like bunnies?*"

"You do love that term, don't you?"

"I love what it means." He moved between her legs and lifted her hips in his warm hands. He leaned in, and Lucy gasped as he slid into her body. "I could squeal you right now, or make it last," he said.

"Both," Lucy said, greedily.

His delighted grin flashed out. He leaned closer, made a minute adjustment, and Lucy gasped and squealed with abandon.

Paris stayed where he was as she came down. "When you're ready, my lady."

"Lucy. I'm not one of your my-ladies. They get to enjoy you, but I'm the one who loves you."

"And you're the one I love."

That startled her.

"You don't have to say that."

"I don't *have* to do anything. I didn't *have* to go back to the island. I don't *have* to come to the island the next time you are there. But I will. Even Lore Mor Arlodh won't stop me. Even that scary milady of his won't frighten me away. I will be with you when I can. When you go back to your other life, I'll be here waiting to love you when we're together again."

"I—"

He leaned forward and kissed her, and Lucy's mind went off to its favourite place, where her favourite person, her puzzling, beloved halfling, dedicated himself to her delight because it was his delight, too.

Later on, sated, and with Paris defused for a while, she lay back dreamily in the shallows of the cascade pool.

London and Kin came down with baby Lara, and Kin sat and fed her child while Paris and London submerged in the pool.

"You got him happy again," Kin observed.

"No, he just *is* happy. He's accepted himself."

The other girl raised one eyebrow and then leaned over and kissed Lucy's shoulder.

Bubbles of life ran through her.

"Nice, eh?" Kin said.

"Very lovely, but I'm a man's woman," Lucy said, laughing.

"Not asking you to play. It's just fun to tease you." Kin's impish mouth quivered.

"Hmm. Do you ever play with Paris, Kin?"

"Mm. I do. I did. He's sweet, but for now, I just play with London." She shook her head. "Never expected that."

Lucy laughed. "Do any of us ever expect what happens to us?"

Kin rocked her baby. "This one will be crawling about soon."

"Really?"

"Mm."

"Are you going to have more?"

"Maybe. Depends on if we feel like making one."

"You and London?"

Kin looked startled and shrugged. Then she looked across to the deeper water. "London. Yes," she said.

"I can hold Lara if you want to go to him," Lucy offered.

Kin handed her over. "Never mind if you get babby loves. It's just Lara playing." She slid out into the water and vanished.

Lucy cuddled the little girl, utterly contented. Lara was babbling and looking up at her with eyes the colour of Indian tea.

The scent of wallflowers alerted Lucy to Mama Tam's arrival. She patted the rock beside her with her free hand, but Tam leaned over and kissed her brow. A feeling of loving protection came over her, rippling like a creek in spring.

"Hello . . . um, greet you, Tam," she said.

"Give me that babby now, sweet. Mistress Lorelei has brought you a gown, and she's waiting up the slope for you. Here . . ." She ran a motherly hand over Lucy's hair, and it dried. "A colleen chose my lad Finn," she remarked.

Waterfolk were prone to non-sequiturs, but Lucy caught that one. Finn must be one of the sons she shared with Liam.

"Is that a good thing?"

"The pride in him is as high as his —"

"TMI! TMI!" Lucy hastily handed Lara to the water maid and fled up the slope.

Getting ready for a May Day Ball *over there* was nothing like dressing for a dance in Sydney. Lucy slipped into the gown Lorelei had brought, a deep green covered with wreaths of blossom and drifting petals.

"It's may bloom!" she exclaimed, enchanted.

"I had it made for a May Day Ball, but I have a new one now. Have you defused that water lad of yours?"

"We fucked like bunnies," Lucy said.

Lorelei smoothed her lavender-coloured tunic and said, "So did we. I needed Augie sedated to get him into the appropriate clothes. He was all for going in his camp gear. Is Paris really going to go in his skin?"

"If that's what he wants."

"This is what he wants," Paris said, stepping into view.

Lucy jumped. She supposed it was simply the reverse of the way fay set out walking and then vanished.

She turned to face him squarely, and they surveyed one another with interest. Paris reached out and stroked the green gown. "Braeside wool. The McTavish flock, I think." He rubbed the cloth between finger and thumb.

"What's that you're wearing?" Lucy asked, admiring him.

He looked down at himself. "Mama Tam got her man Liam's sister to make these for me."

"You look handsome," Lucy said.

"That's a set of leprechaun britches, and I think the top's a courting shirt," Lorelei put in.

Paris said, "I call cousin with the gossoons at Blarney Edge, so I can wear these on account of green blood."

"I see. That is, I don't, but I expect I will, one day. Are your parents coming?"

"Maybe. Mammy's got a teg man under the falls. My father stayed with Liam for some poteen."

"We'd better go," Lorelei said hastily.

CHAPTER TWENTY-EIGHT: QUEEN OF THE MAY

Lucy Tan, 2020, Over there

Lucy's impression of *over there* had been one of simplicity. She found the castle, where the May Day Ball was held, an utterly new experience.

It was a literal castle, but, unlike the ones she'd seen in holiday brochures and documentaries, it was clearly a home as well.

August and Lorelei walked straight up the sweeping steps, but Lucy lingered. "Paris, do you mind if we stop for a while and watch the people coming in?"

"It's a fine sight," he said.

"Oh, look!" Lucy was enchanted to see carriages drawing into the courtyard. Ladies dressed in ballgowns descended, shaped like full-blown roses. A flock of young women in clear, bright colours ran by in a patter of slippers and a toss of ribboned curls, and six men in kilts and plaids marched up the castle steps playing their pipes.

One of them, to Lucy's amusement, was Cameron Dougal. He caught her eye and gave her an outrageous wink.

"Are they part of the dance band?" Lucy asked Paris.

"I've not been to a ball before," he reminded her.

Lucy looked about with delight. The gown Lorelei had lent her swirled fluidly around her ankles, and Paris had made her a wreath of may flowers, bound with silk ribbon.

Excitement ran through her as she heard music drifting from the battlements.

Fair-haired men with patrician features passed, and one stopped to bow to her.

"Greetings, fair lady. The Queen of the May, I assume?"

Lucy got into character and dropped a curtsey. "I am! I am! Thank you, sir. Might I know your name?"

"Godfrey de Courcey at your service, ma'am. Will you save me a dance?"

Lucy glanced at Paris and saw he was smiling at Godfrey.

"Greet you, man. Need a hug?"

"Not tonight, Paris, but thank you." The young man stood back. "I almost didn't know you with your pants on. Er — are they your pants?"

Lucy put her arm around Paris. "They're his pants. He *chose* to wear them. And yes, I'll dance with you, Master de Courcey."

A large hand clamped down on the fair man's shoulder and shifted him aside. Its owner confronted Paris.

"We meet again, water lad. And again, you're clothed."

Lucy looked up into a strong-featured face. The man wore a dark suit, and he had his other arm possessively around a strawberry blonde dressed in shimmering mother-of-pearl. "You and your wife are also clothed," she said to the seaman.

He gave her his haughtiest look. "*Chons da,* May Queen."

He strode away, but his wife turned and winked at Lucy.

"He said good luck to you. He must be feeling . . ." The last of her words faded as her man whisked her away.

Two pretty elf women paused to gawk at Paris. One laughed, and Lucy was momentarily annoyed, until she came up, hands outstretched. "Paris! I've missed you at the falls. Will you be there tomorrow?"

"Not tomorrow, but one day soon," he said.

"A hug then?"

He hesitated. "Go on," Lucy said.

The woman stepped up into his arms, and they embraced.

"Lovely, isn't he?" the other woman said to Lucy.

"Yes, he really is. Are you one of his my-ladies, too? I mean, do you play with him?"

"Not since I found my match last year. Phillie still favours him."

"So do I," Lucy said. She went on smiling as Paris released the elf and his gaze fixed back on her.

He reached for her hand.

"Maybe we'd better go in," she ventured, but a woman with chestnut curls down her back stopped in a swirl of gold skirts, pulling her escort to a halt. She stared at Paris, and her mouth dropped open in an O of surprise.

Another one of his my-ladies . . . I'll have to get used to this.

"You can talk to her, or hug her," she said gently.

Paris let go of Lucy's hand and stepped forward to the beauty in gold. "Greet you, Mistress Peckerdale. Master Peckerdale."

"May the Great Bogle fly away wid me!" her man exclaimed in a marked brogue. He had a crooked mouth and a voice like honey. "Darlin' Yvanne . . . did ye ever see the like? A water lad at a ball! An' wearin' britches!"

"Paris!" The woman gestured in the air and was suddenly holding a set of softly glowing pipes. "I have these still," she said. She came in closer, leaned out against her wide skirts and kissed him on the cheek. "Is your friend coming, too?"

"No, my lady. London is with Kin and their babby at the falls. Mammy and my father might come." Paris turned and beckoned to Lucy. "This is my Lucy, my love, my Queen of the May."

The young woman bent to offer her hand. "Greet you, Lucy. Paris gave me these pipes when I was feeling sad and reminded me of how beautiful life can be." Her gaze passed over Lucy's gown in friendly interest. "And you look beautiful in your May Day gown—"

"So do you, and so I should," Lucy said. She let go and held out her skirts, waltzing herself in a circle. "After all these years, I have everything I need, and just for today, I really am the Queen of the May!"

YOU MAY ALSO ENJOY THE FOLLOWING FROM EXTASY BOOKS INC:

Peter and Pia
Lark Westerly

Excerpt

Art School was fun.

Barbie, flushed with satisfaction at having finally broken free of the placid certainties of Windhill, moved in at Lady Lydia Appledore House, a respectable boarding hostel where students and young workers lived. Her brother lived with a classmate on the floor above for the first year. Then, as his medical studies progressed, he and his friend moved closer to the university and the hospital where he was doing his practical training.

"You'll be all right, Barbie?"

"Of course I will. I'm not a kiddy." She was nearly twenty-one. Her parents and Jacobi had wanted her to go home after her course ended, but Barbie had started a new one, which was more exciting. She worked part-time as a model for one of the teachers, wearing a playsuit so the students could see her limbs. She'd also been asked to pose for a life drawing class, but of course, she'd said no.

She almost wrote to Jacobi and told him about it, but in the end, she didn't. He'd be upset.

He came on one of his occasional visits soon after that, and they drove to Melbourne and went dancing.

Then Jacobi had to spoil it by asking when she was coming home.

"This is home, for now," she said. She indicated Lady Lydia Appledore House, which was inevitably known as LadyLyddy by its occupants. "Would you like to come in for coffee?"

"What exactly do you mean by coffee?"

"Coffee. In the common-room. What did you think I meant?"

Jacobi thanked her and declined. He said he'd stay in Johnny's room for the night and drive home in the morning. He got out of the car.

Barbie was confused until she realised Jacobi thought Johnny was still at LadyLyddy.

That was awkward.

"Are you going to tell my parents?"

Jacobi looked surprised. "I don't even see your parents from one week to the next. You should tell them, though. Or come home."

They didn't part on the best of terms.

Barbie saw the new boy arrive. He got out of a car driven by a middle-aged lady. She got out, too, and passed him a bag.

She reached up to kiss his cheek. "You'll be okay, Peter. Let us know if you need anything."

"I'll be all right. Thanks for the ride. I've got to learn how to drive these fucking things."

"Peter—"

"Sorry. Keep forgetting."

"You had two years to get the language right."

He lifted a shoulder. "Yes, but that's a while ago. Bye, anyway, Prue."

She drove off, and the boy stood looking a bit lost.

He was tall, with black hair and an arresting face. His skin was a strong shade of olive.

Italian, like Julia Conti.

Barbie wanted to paint him, but what he'd said to the lady made her doubtful about approaching him.

Maybe he doesn't speak English very well.

She approached him with caution. "Hello. I'm Barbara. Barbie. Do you need any help with your things?"

He looked her over and smiled. He had a slightly crooked mouth, and his eyes were an odd colour, almost blue, but stronger and brighter. Turquoise, maybe. "Barbie. Are you human?"

She laughed. "Yes. Aren't you?"

"No."

He was odd, all right.

"Come in, and I'll show you where to register."

"I've got a room fixed," he said.

"Do you know where?"

"Third floor, number sixteen. I got the key from Prue last week."

She was impressed. The third floor was reserved for working people. It wasn't a dorm, and some of the rooms even had their own bathrooms, or so she'd heard.

"I'll help you find it," she said.

They went up the stairs and located the room. The boy touched the door, and it swung open.

Can't have been locked . . . oh, wait . . . did he conjure that?

"Want to come in?" he asked.

"No."

She did, rather.

"I'd better not," she added.

"Oh. No harm."

"Of course not, but it's not really done."

"My name's Peter Peckerdale," he said, holding out a massive hand.

She shook. His hand was warm, and he smelled of fresh

grass.

An elf? Could be.

"Maybe I'll see you around, Peter."

She peeped past him into the room. It had lovely light. It was much bigger than her little place with its shared bathroom where two of the other girls left their stockings and under-things hanging in the bathroom to dry.

She put away envy and went downstairs.

Barbie blamed Jacobi for what happened after that. She knew it was unfair, but if he hadn't been so stiff and disapproving after the dance, she might have gone home at the end of the term. Also, she blamed him for being an elf and for giving her an insight into that secret world of conjuring and what she thought of as magic. The elves she knew were nice people. Even Jacobi was nice when he wasn't carrying on like a Victorian papa. He was only two years older than she was, so why did he have to be so stiff?

She thought Peter Peckerdale was an elf, too, and that made her feel safe. It was Jacobi's fault for being the way he was.

Peter was an odd mixture. She'd thought he was at least her age, but he said he was just eighteen and had enough years, whatever that meant. He talked like a navvy. His swearing bothered her, though he never blasphemed. In other ways, he was quaintly old-fashioned.

They had coffee in the common-room sometimes, although he didn't seem to like it much. They went to the pictures, and he held her hand. He didn't know how to drive, so she taught him in Johnny's car.

Peter and Johnny got along well. Johnny said he was an interesting specimen and speculated on whether he had green blood.

Peter said he didn't, but that he sometimes went a bit green when he got embarrassed.

Barbie saw no evidence of that. Peter didn't seem to care what other people thought of him.

Then Johnny asked for a sample of Peter's blood because Jacobi had told him things about blood and immunity.

Peter gave it to him, but he refused to go into the hospital for tests. "Not fucking likely."

He was looking for work, so Barbie took him to the art school and introduced him to the teacher who'd wanted models. After that, she used to find sketches of Peter's face and hands pinned to easels and gracing portfolios. He was popular among the bohemian set, who didn't mind his language. He was graceful in an odd way, and he could stand in a pose for a long time without complaint.

She heard he did some of the special poses for the life drawing and was surprised at how oddly conflicted she felt. He had every right to earn some extra money, and he was a wonderful figure to draw, but he seemed so casual about it all.

"Aren't you embarrassed?"

"Why would I be? I have a cloth over my bits, mostly."

"Peter!"

"You know I've got fucking bits. So have you. Nice ones." He reached for her chest, and she smacked his hand away.

"Don't."

This was happening too often for her peace of mind.

"Don't you like me?"

"You know I do." She thought about Jacobi, who had never, ever reached for her chest.

"No harm," he said. He looked dejected.

"Not for you. Girls have to be careful."

"I'd be careful. I give good warmth." He kissed her, and she felt the warmth of his arms. She relaxed against him. Then he patted her bottom, and she jumped away. "No, Peter."

"Don't you like being loved?"

That startled her. He sounded sad.

"You're a dear, and maybe someday, but not now."

ABOUT THE AUTHOR

Lark Westerly lives on the island state of Tasmania.

One of her favourite occupations is weaving stories about the mix of fairy and human characters in the *Fairy in the Bed, Red Cat* and *Pixie Grip* series.